JASPER CLIFF

First published 2024 by
FREMANTLE PRESS

Fremantle Press Inc. trading as Fremantle Press
PO Box 158, North Fremantle, Western Australia, 6159
fremantlepress.com.au

Cover photographs by Jody D'Arcy, 'Pilbara Rock', jodydarcy.com;
Ian Hitchcock, istockphoto.com
Designed by Nada Backovic, nadabackovic.com
Printed and bound by IPG

NATIONAL LIBRARY OF AUSTRALIA
A catalogue record for this book is available from the National Library of Australia

ISBN 9781760993498 (paperback)
ISBN 9781760993504 (ebook)

GOVERNMENT OF WESTERN AUSTRALIA
Department of Local Government, Sport and Cultural Industries
lotterywest

Fremantle Press is supported by the State Government through the Department of Local Government, Sport and Cultural Industries.

Fremantle Press respectfully acknowledges the Whadjuk people of the Noongar nation as the Traditional Owners and Custodians of the land where we work in Walyalup.

JASPER CLIFF

JOSH KEMP

FREMANTLE PRESS

Josh Kemp is an author of Australian gothic and crime fiction. His debut novel, *Banjawarn*, was the winner of the 2021 Dorothy Hewett Award, the 2022 Ned Kelly Award for Best Debut Crime Fiction and the 2023 Western Australian Premier's Prize for Best Emerging Writer. *Jasper Cliff* is his second novel. He lives in the south-west of Western Australia but finds himself drawn, over and over again, to the red dirt of the state's north.

This novel is set on the traditional lands of the Nyamal, Wajarri and Yamatji peoples. I wish to pay my respects to their Elders past and present.

This is, always was and always will be Aboriginal land.

1

Toby presses deeper into the shade cast by the minni ritchi tree. He has seen few lush as this one, outstretching so many shiraz-coloured limbs. Usually, they are gaunt and spindly. He tries to imagine the tree's taproot, plunging metres down into some hidden aquifer deep in hot rock.

He peers down at the broken granite outcrop. Little can be known of what came before by standing here now. These were scraps by which only snatches of other lives could be gleaned. Mostly, they had left behind damage. Where the ochre rock has been chipped by tools blunted back to stone themselves by now. The only evidence of their passing is how they've wounded the earth.

He peels the faded black cap from his head to paw at the sweat on his brow and turns his eyes to the fierce sky, as if this could be the source of his sustenance. Some heavy, pitiless aquifer above; his taproot always reaching but never gaining hold. Toby wants to escape all this damage but now it's too hot to move.

The giddiness whacks him out of nowhere. He's got the heat-dizzies. Pushed it too far, been out here too long. The car becomes something to aim for, the only thing to hold his path true; the only thing to stop him trailblazing into a perpetuity of wattle scurf.

Once back in the cab, he twists his key in the ignition and redirects the fan so the aircon hits him right in the face. He smiles as the blood throbs in both ears. Then peers out at the world baking through the windshield and he can pretend it was never so close to claiming him, body and soul. He's never experienced heat like this before. It would be so easy to just give over to it.

Toby listens to the engine lurch back to life and he loops around in the dirt to make for the station road. Now he's roused himself from the watery world of mirage outside, he does wonder what keeps him fixed in place; he wonders what keeps him from leaving the cold cab of the car behind and cutting a line out into the mulga.

The answer is simple. Mum and Dad, he thinks. *Hell, even Lachlan*. His family has always been his taproot.

This late in the day, he can't believe it isn't cooling down yet. This coming summer might cook the earth like a roast chicken but perhaps this country can endure whatever awaits. After all, it's survived so much already. The planet's tectonic tantrums, broiling summers and ice ages, and the whitefellas – its greatest challenge of all. Whitefellas like himself searching for what can only be found in the clutch of mulga.

Toby goes vacant and the country streams all sides and before him, and it fills him up. It reaves whatever he might've been before and he becomes only the magnitude of *it*. This baked-dry thing which has endured the volcanic rupturing of the planet settling itself into place, shouldering hungrily from a primordial ocean, just so it can see the sun.

Hardly aware he's smiling again, bright as the scalding earth out there, he looks back down at the station road and sees the perentie just a few metres ahead. Toby gasps with surprise and plants the brake. All happening so fast, he wonders if he's still a bit heat-slugged because now he's seeing everything happen in slow motion.

The perentie blinks at the Prado screaming towards it through a carmine-red curtain of dust but doesn't move. When in danger, it roots itself to the baking dirt road. Realising he's not going to straddle the goanna but plough its head into the gravel, Toby pulls on the steering wheel too hard. The cab tilts ever so slightly but he doesn't feel the world tip off its axis. Instead, he watches a falcon swing in and claw at the perentie.

The two lock claws for the briefest moment. Falcon and goanna. As the Prado swings out of control, Toby's relieved to see he'll miss them both, and he wonders how long this battle has been playing out. How far these skirmishes can be traced across the country's itchy, rumpled skin.

Toby's sweating so much he can feel any purchase he once had on the steering wheel loosen. Watches the wattle blossom sprinkle the windshield. The car clumps to a halt on the roadside, nudging a gaunt minni ritchi tree.

He laughs so hard it sounds like a shrieking stranger is hiding in the back seat. He quickly rests the engine, cracks open the driver's side door and steps out. Checks the sky but the falcon is nowhere to be seen, having coasted away. The perentie is watching him from the middle of the road after narrowly escaping the falcon's claws, still hasn't budged, not even after the Prado nearly hit it and then skidded up against the scrub in a rampage of pink chalk dust.

The goanna finally turns away from the beaming stranger – just another whitefella passing through – and drags itself, over a metre long, off into the rock litter. Toby trails after it, the air so hot it's like drawing in breath just millimetres above a campfire. With the sun in decline, the perentie leads Toby across primeval ground lit red but capped with black stones.

He loses sight of the goanna only when he looks up and sees the granite outcrop snuggled between stands of minni ritchi. These rocks too have been chipped at, battered and cracked and hewn. Refolded for purpose. The Chinese prospectors were all through this country, only thirty kilometres west of Cue. As prolific gardeners, they often sought shade to foster their crops. Sought shade in country where there was so little. And then took full advantage of it.

But now there's only ruins, same as the last lot he visited. A still-standing stone wall, pieced together from granite bits, fetched from the land all about. Toby kneels and stares at it. How might a visitor pass through without leaving a scar like this?

He's just stood to go, not hearing the scuttle of the goanna as it returns to the liquid hot heart of the country, like water trailing back to the boiling aquifer below, possibly preparing for its next Herculean battle with the falcon, when something catches Toby's eye. Away from the dreck of the garden granites is a lone orange boulder. It's enormous, bigger than the Prado. A lonely moon having crashed to earth. A sole shrub fingering from its shoulder.

'Check you out,' Toby says.

When he approaches, his gaiters crunching in the stony litter, he sees there's a hole in the side of the lone rock. From back here, it looks like a mouth. Looks like it might say something to the visitor if it could string any words together.

Despite the heat bearing down, Toby presses up against the weight of the orange granite. He kneels slowly, can feel the sweat forming a wet outline of his sunglasses where they sit unsteadily on his face. He peers into the mouth.

Something alive. It shifts around, swaddled within, at having the intrusive human stink fill its burrow. He can't imagine what might live inside this huge block of cooking rock and it's too dark in there to make out. So he peels off his sunnies and presses deeper, closer.

'Knock, knock.'

Whatever it is shuffles around restlessly now.

'Who's there?'

At first, he suspects it's one of his seizures. *Oh fuck no, not now*. But then realises this is different. Can't blame it on his epilepsy. Not this time.

He's been so good lately with keeping on top of his medication. Still, the edges of his vision crackle with static. Can't see it right because his body has started to spasm. Surprised spit jettisons from his mouth. Out of the corner of his eye, he sees a shape knife from the aperture of orange rock, what looks like something emerging and resting its scaly hand on his chest and—

It's night now. After the heat of the day, the cold is unbearable, though the fat boy battles his way through the mulga. The voices of others so close, Cantonese by the sounds of it. The fat boy tries to be quiet. Can't bark out in agony though the pain is blinding. He weaves his way through leafless wattles, clutching at the enormous weight through his droopy cotton shirt.

He collapses here, at the base of the granite outcrop, and the fat boy knows he can flee no further. The pain-sweat has already soaked through the felt hat on his head and he flings it off into the scrub and only now lets out a growl of despair.

The boy breathes hard, whimpering intakes of starlight, and looks up at the folds of moon-hot granite looking back down at him. For the briefest moment, all of the boy's fears are dispelled, as if forming some wordless covenant with the watching rocks. The boy rubs both hands over his massively distended belly and it's apparent the boy isn't just fat, but his stomach has swollen like an infected limb which needs amputating.

He gives one last cry of horror before his long johns darken with blood. The soft granite absorbs his pain, laves the sweat on his brow with a breath of wind. The fat, crying boy can almost hear the rock's gentle voice telling him he is safe, that there is nothing to fear in this place. Telling him he should not resist what is happening, only that he should let it happen.

And he does. At first there's no sound in the boy's gory long johns. He reaches with fresh alarm through the muddy stuff below and finally shows the granite outcrop the infant which just emerged.

Not a boy but a girl. Girl and child still joined by a sausage link of flesh and yet one is much quieter than the other.

Too quiet.

It's only when the girl peers back at the moonlit granite, eyes beseeching, that another rush of breeze stirs the wattles and, finally, the baby cries out. The girl whimpers back with relief and clutches the slimy child to the chest of her cotton shirt.

It won't be long now before the others hear the baby's wailing, too loud to stifle in the cold night, so the girl with the cropped hair just lounges back in the rocks, in this her child's birthplace, and peers up at the curves of the granite outcrop, thinking this would be an ideal and shady spot for her family's next crop.

Toby senses the back of his head clapping viciously against the ground but can barely feel it. Finally, the vision fades from his mind's eye and now there's only the orange boulder towering above him. Its mouth or anus or all-seeing eye peering back down at him, sympathetic.

Toby glares up into the boiling sky and rakes his elbow across the saliva which has heaped across his chin and neck. Then scuttles back from the hole, in case it shows him some other truth, buried in the deep shelving of granite.

Once back to his feet, he hangs there staring, and can't be sure he didn't imagine the whole thing. But when he looks back at the garden granites, he sees everything is almost the same as his vision; perhaps only a century has passed since the Chinese girl gave birth here.

Toby's momentary fear, mindless as it is, passes with the hot wind which wends off the baked ground. It's a gift, he realises slowly, suddenly ebullient. To have been shown what he was shown. He returns to the eye in the boulder now and leans against the cooking surface of granite and lounges there.

From here he can see a nest of mulga all interlocked to form a high eyrie above the soft bedding of purple everlastings. He watches the falcon swing back to its place up there, possibly just returned from its latest conflict with the perentie. The bird of prey's periscopic eye able to see so much and so far, but perhaps not as much as Toby has just seen.

2

Rainy days, so few and far between out this way, always remind him of what he did to Ricky Muswell.

It's a surprise to Glen that he really doesn't think about it more often. Possibly a surprise to think there might be something wrong with him for not feeling so bad about it. Hell, he doesn't even dream about it no more.

Ten years later. Ten years since he heard Muswell die in the dirt. It's been so long it could be someone else's crime. A memory of murder he inherited.

He zips up the front of his shorts, savouring the warm drizzle descending on the side of this lonesome road. The Hamersley Range curves gently twenty k's or so in the distance, some of the peaks so high the clouds scrape those iron domes with their marshmallowy bellies. Glen feels the heat implode in his knee as he slides back in behind the steering wheel of his ute, eager to escape the sludge of crimson road fast turning to mud. He rubs at the knee but this just makes it worse. Must be acting up after being locked in the same position during his five-hour drive this morning.

Gettin' old, ya silly bugger.

Yes, when he looks in the mirror each morning now, he can pick out where the white hairs are scrawling like pale millipedes above his ears. He'll be grey all over in just a few years.

Slamming the door behind him and cranking the engine again, Glen thinks about the look on Muswell's face just before Glen brought the star picket down into his eye socket. It was the look of someone who never really thought they would die a young man. As if the promise of more life was so spellbinding, the idea that it might ever be snatched away could only plainly be a lie.

Lost in memories now, Glen almost doesn't see the long road ahead of him, all turning to mud the colour of pinot noir. Though the engine rumbles, he doesn't make a move. Can only remember the satisfying, sick thudding sound the star picket made against Muswell's skull.

A decade ago, a mate had got him the job right on the fringe of the Ripon Hills for some bigwig mining company, helmed by one of the same greedy pricks who kicked up a stink when the Rudd Government wanted to slog them with a super-profits-tax. Glen hadn't been fond of their politics, but he needed the money. After Layla came home from work one day to their Joondanna white brick unit and told him she'd been fucking her yoga instructor – Lorenzo; many years younger than Glen – he'd wanted out of the city as fast as possible before the divorce proceedings could begin.

He'd never met Muswell before but the two of them were tasked with driving down a crimson road as lonely as the one Glen sits idle on now. They were given maps and herbariums and lists of endangered animals and critters, with photographs alongside to show a clear example of what they were looking for.

The mining company had its eye on this particular swatch of hummock grassland, and it was Glen and Muswell's job to pace out the fence lines, through the Kingsmill's mallees and endless stretches of spinifex, and if they found any of the endangered flora or fauna species, they had to take a reading of the exact spot on GPS and report back to base over radio as soon as possible.

It was child's play. Anyone who'd bailed out of high school way too early could do it with their eyes taped shut, and Glen came to suspect that's exactly why Muswell had got the job. He was a talker, that much was clear as soon as Glen got in the work ute and they started driving. Straight out of Rockingham, only a year after quitting TAFE and chucking in an apprenticeship, the little ginger weasel seemed bizarrely self-confident. Glen watched the road unfold like a ribbon, watched the ragged bulk of the Ripon Hills inch closer, shining gold and sometimes with a tinsel of crimson wound through their slopes, and with each ghost gum they passed, he wondered how Muswell had ended up like this, as if he had the whole fucken world in the palm of his hand while having achieved literally nothing in his life at the ripe old age of twenty-one.

Glen had just decided it was a symptom of young people these days. They faked it until they made it. Or didn't make it, more often than not. But that's when Muswell started in on him. Looking back on it now, Glen wonders if Muswell targeted him for his reticence. His unwillingness to join in with Muswell's nasty banter about how there were too many Māoris in the Pilbara these days. So Muswell turned on him. Asked him how old he was. Glen stupidly answered, 'Turned fifty this year. The big five-O.'

It was a mistake. 'Just a little bubby, aren't ya?' Muswell cackled. 'Can ya still get it up or what? Or is that later when ya go limp all the time?'

Glen didn't answer.

'Well, what are we gunna call ya then?'

Glen. Just Glen will do.

'Gramps? Pops? Eh, Pops? I like that.' His laughter filled the ute with shards of glass. 'Nah, I know. We'll call ya *Bubs*. Coz ya just a widdle bubby is all.'

This went on all afternoon. While they set up their tents in the rain, while they huddled in the canvas five or so metres apart, even after Glen had tried to burrow into his sleeping bag to get away from the mongrel's raving through the thin walls. He liked to have a dig as well as any other man, but this was hellish. Being stuck with this fucker's endless nattering, picking cruelty.

When Glen woke later in the dark, roused by the gurgling snores, he did consider, for the briefest moment, unzipping his tent and creeping over quietly and opening Muswell's tent and then jamming the pillow across Muswell's face, clamping it hard over his mouth. He imagined the satisfying whimper below as the loudmouth, smart-arse, cocky little cunt realised what was happening to him, and that he couldn't worm his way out of this one. Not this fucken time.

It wasn't the first time he'd let the thought come sneaking. Couldn't recall the first time he'd fantasised about taking a life. There'd been all those birds and mice when he was a tyke, digging graves behind the back shed, stomping back over the disturbed earth under the lemon tree to hide his grim little secrets. But the thought of taking a human life had always glistened with the most terrible promise. He only needed a reason. Please God – one day – just give him a reason.

Glen was awake for some time, considering it. The throb of energy coursing through him like when he was a tyke and he clenched his fingers and saw the crushed grey mouse spurting blood in his fist.

But throttling Muswell in that tent and killing house mice were two very different things. Apples and oranges. Even when Dad caught him with that dead pigeon in a spit of feathers, Glen had noted his father's alarm, but it hadn't gone any further than that.

'Just an accident, was it mate?' his father had asked, nodded to himself and then quickly fled inside. 'Better get rid of it before ya mum sees, eh?'

He would never get away with this. The mining company had sent them out together. It'd be too obvious if only one of them returned. Plus, just the thought of the hole he'd have to dig for Muswell wore him out, and they'd only given him one of those pissy little camp shovels. So Glen rolled over in his sleeping bag and, hoping he worked up a solid snore once he went under to contend with Muswell's, he watched the tent walls ripple until he fell back asleep.

Glen starts, jolting back to the here and now. He tries to imagine if he had suffocated Muswell that first night. Instead of what happened a couple of days after arriving at the grasslands. Again, a decade later, the feel of the star picket is so clear, its unyielding muscle, denting Muswell's skull and sending jets of blood spurting across the spinifex.

He looks through the windscreen now, half expecting to see the man's spectre step out of the black stands of mulga, his lopsided head flecked with pieces of bone. Glen smacks his dry lips together. Thinking about what he did to Muswell has left him parched, thirsty for the feel of blood speckled across his face again.

He cracks open the driver's side door again and now the drizzle is so faint he can barely feel it. In the back seat of the Triton, he always stashes a handy ten-litre tank of water in case he ever breaks down on the side of the road. It's something he learned from the locals. Even if the car's heart did quit in the fiery heat, a road train or mining ute would be along in a few hours, a day or two, a week. Still, best not to be caught out waiting by the broken-down car on a forty-two-degree day without anything to drink.

Glen twists the nozzle, watches the water fill his plastic bottle. Having the passenger door hanging open, blocking his view of the Hamersley Range, leaves him feeling itchy, restless. Exposed.

After all, that's when ya gave it to Muswell, he thinks. *When he least expected it. When the little bastard's back was turned.*

He watches the mud road below the open door, able to measure the seconds of each intake and exhale of breath. Surely, it's the warm rain on his skin making him itch like mad, not the feeling of being watched from the scrub.

Glen surprises himself by slamming the door all of a sudden, straightening. But when he peers across the road, water bottle clenched in one hand, he sees it's only a Shorthorn bull watching him. Not Muswell's ghost. Still, the bull could've been a worry. If it had decided to charge him while he was filling his water bottle, it had enough muscle to crush him between the cab and open door. Can imagine the sound of his ribs shattering inward, lancing vital organs.

'Gorn, you! Fucken git!' Glen calls out, waving both hands in the drizzle.

Behind the bull, Glen now spots a nondescript cattle yard. Must be fifty years old, just sitting there, slowly falling in on itself; the bull trots through it on its panicked return to the valley plain.

Glen walks right across the road waving his arms – the mud squelching with each step until he reaches the crossing planks, all lined with the trails of termites – and now he's alone once again, he can breathe easier. The slightest tease of mizzle touches his bottom lip. He's always preferred solitude. Maybe that's why he took such relish in dispensing with Muswell. Because he wanted to be out there near the Ripon Hills all by himself, unassailed by Muswell's unending babble. He'd only ever tasted blood the few times he'd cut himself at home with the kitchen knife, quickly popping the fingertip into his mouth. But there was so much more of Muswell's – metallic but also, somehow, earthy.

Am I a vampire or somethin'?

His loud laugh only dies in his throat when he hears the hissing. Not how he'd imagine a snake would hiss; this is closer to a growl. Sounds as if it's coming from a much heftier creature, something with a lot more muscle behind it. Glen looks down at the dark bands encircling the shiny line of it, the python's head jet black and gleaming like a seal freshly breached from the sea.

Most of the black-headed python has unravelled from a mud hole below the wood posts and it's rearing only a little, coiling back on itself and stiffening to see the human trespasser so close. Glen can sense the space separating him from the python thicken as his blood thickens. The petrifying majesty of this moment, his eyes locked with its eyes. This thing which has only known mulga and valley plain and the blood of bush mouse.

The truth is resolute, can never be kept buried for long; he'd got properly jacked from doing away with Muswell. A feverish memory of how he'd stumbled afterwards, blood-drunk into the night, towards a broken line of distant hills and he could sense it all. Every fibre in every chunk of basalt clanking underfoot. Every seed of spinifex shaken free and lost on the welter of wind. He found himself clambering the side of a lone outcrop in the dark. The stars like pricks of stainless steel, each with their own hastening pulse.

Finally, Glen was a part of the earth. He knew what bits and pieces needed to fit together, and where it was coming apart at the seams, and finally understood his place within it. The lowly pawn on the chessboard. And the chessboard was right before him, darkening eastward. The unfathomable stretch of desert. That expanse beyond comprehension.

Glen starts, and stares into the cattle yard. Must be getting old. All this reminiscence, these unstoppable memories. He guesses, up until a decade ago, he'd always been a city boy. Had always thought human ingenuity and endeavour had shaped the universe. Until that night he stood on a platform of high basalt, caked in the blood of another human being, and faced the desert.

He can sense that same darkened expanse in the python at his feet now and realises he's taken another step towards it without thinking. The black-headed python stiffens harder and growls again. His breath hurries, lusty. 'Gorn then,' Glen whispers.

When the black-headed python sinks its fangs into his calf

muscle, Glen's alive like he hasn't been for ten years. All this time stumbling around in a daze, wondering nonchalantly if someone will come knocking on his door one day and claim they knew what he'd done to Ricky Muswell. Perhaps he'd supposed he could never recapture that feeling of weightlessness, him and the sprawling desert, a grain of sand watching the ocean creep towards it.

But here it is now, feeling the python's fangs buried deep in his muscle and he groans with pleasure. If the thing had evolved to deposit venom into its prey, he'd be throbbing with poison right now.

The python retracts its fangs and quickly loops in on itself. It hula-hoops around some spinifex and slides back into its hole below the fence post. Glen gasps, ecstatic. Trembles with caliginous energy. He peers down to inspect the two tiny puncture marks on calf muscle, like Dracula visited him in the night.

Glen wonders if his blood tastes as good as Ricky Muswell's.

Must still be coming down from the high of it all when Glen hears an intrusive car horn in the distance. Not too far away either. He quickly pivots back to the road, wondering if he didn't park the Triton over far enough. Wondering, with horror, if someone had witnessed this most sacred act which just transpired. Glen stumbles back towards the track, an almost libidinal throb in his calf where the python tasted his blood.

'What the holy hell?' he mutters.

Not sure how he hadn't seen it when he first pulled up, though he is getting old after all, and his eyesight isn't what it used to be. He spent his sixtieth a couple of months earlier drinking with Shrubb, putting away a whole carton of Emu Export between them. Hadn't told Shrubb it was his birthday, didn't want to make a fuss. He was more worried about June finding out they'd been drinking, feared she'd show up at the front flywire with a star picket in her hands to chase them away from the bottle.

There's a car in the shoulder right down the other end of the mud road, a smudge of white under some shaggy mulga. He can see now the hazard lights are flashing, painfully bright on this grey day. Glen returns to the Triton, only giving himself a moment to glance back at the abandoned cattle yard and yearn for the return of the black-headed python. He guns it down the road, painting the Triton's sides with more sludge, and then slows again once he reaches the Falcon.

For a moment he sees Ricky Muswell, again, standing beside the flashing lights of the car, head caved-in and grinning with what teeth still remained in his gob.

But the stranger is a bit older than Muswell had been. Flushed and breathless, both hands planted on his hips, as if he is entitled to rescue. 'Thank God,' he huffs.

'Ya right?' Glen asks with a friendly smile. Can feel his cheeks still glowing. The fang marks still throbbing.

The stranger frowns, gestures to the Falcon. 'What's it look like?'

'If I had to guess? Car troubles?'

Clicks his fingers. 'Got it in one.'

The thought scythes through Glen's mind, so quick it's almost imperceptible; he wonders if anyone knows the stranger is out here on his own.

He wonders if the stranger will be missed.

Lachlan stands back and lets the stranger browse under the bonnet. He looks back at the scrub behind him and sees a dead euro lying on its side next to some lofty mulga, the tree limbs holding onto the stripped pieces of a black plastic bag; must've blown from someone's car or one of the mine sites around here.

He hates to turn back to the Falcon. Every time he does, the dread scrambles up into his throat like a rat looking for a warm spot to nest. 'Sorry again,' he tells the bloke. 'I'm not good with cars. You might be good with cars, I dunno.' Cuts himself off once he realises he's rambling.

The stranger straightens, looks at him. 'She's cooked.'

'What's that mean?'

'A stone's gone through ya radiator. It's rare, but it can happen, especially on roads like this mongrel.' He gesticulates back down the mud track. 'Probly no way ya woulda been able to tell. But coz ya've kept drivin' her, the engine's cooked. Couldn't cool down, see?'

Lachlan watches the bloke's mouth move but doesn't absorb a single word; he bounces on the spot and watches the rain drift over the range. 'So what's that mean? Can you fix it? You got tools in your ute? I don't keep tools with me.'

The stranger watches him, jaw rolling a little. 'I dunno how else plainly I can put this.'

'Put what?'

'Okay.' He clears his throat. 'This. Car. Is. Stuffed.'

Finally, it lands, the cruel meaning only a little delayed this time. He turns back to the Falcon.

'And I mean,' he goes on, 'Like really stuffed. Not just a little stuffed. But properly fucked.'

Lachlan palms at his sweaty face. 'No way.'

'Yes way. I'm real sorry. Ya not goin' anywhere.' Only now does some sympathy glimmer in the man's eyes. 'Look, if ya can get her towed, there's no reason ya can't get a new motor. Ya insurance might even cover it.'

The irritation crackles in Lachlan's voice again. 'Oh yeah? And where am I going to get a fucken tow out here?'

The stranger raises his eyebrows.

'Sorry. Shit's sake. I'm sorry.' He grumbles, looks down the bloody band of road again – the never-ending road. 'This is just the worst possible timing, that's all.'

'Dunno what would be good timin' for ya car crackin' the shits but there ya have it.' He opens two empathetic palms. 'Just don't shoot the messenger and all that.'

'I appreciate you having a look. Thank you.' He looks back at the dead euro, another reflux of dread, the taste of bile. 'Been sitting here over an hour already and I started to freak out that someone might not be along for the rest of the day.'

'It's one of the only roads out to Marble Bar so ya woulda been alright. Eventually. Might've had to wait a day or two but ya woulda had some Roy Hill fucker come through. Ya just lucky ya got such a stand-up bloke like meself.'

He doesn't like the idea that he could've been stuck out here for a whole day, or longer. Now when he looks back and sees the man grin, Lachlan can't help but smile back. 'Thank you, again.' Holds out a hand. 'I'm Lachlan by the way.'

'Glen.'

The shake is almost gentle, not a hint of the hard-man firmness Lachlan was expecting from someone out here.

Lachlan nudges the Falcon with his foot. 'I guess if she's well-and-truly shat it, I might have to ask you for a ride?'

'Nup, ya don't need to ask at all.' Glen rattles his car keys. 'Not gunna abandon a fellow traveller in need. Git ya gear. We'll lob it in the tray.'

Lachlan opens the back door and drags out his suitcase and backpack. Once he glances up at Glen again, noticing the creep of silver along the back of his hairline, the trepidation mutates inside. No longer fixating on Toby, no longer has anything to do with why he drove sixteen hundred kilometres up to the East Pilbara.

He watches Glen open the driver's side door of his Triton and root around in there. Lachlan twists left, then right. Two scarlet-stained euros in the middle of the mud road in the far distance. If Glen were to do anything, even they'd be too far away to see.

Lachlan turns to look at the back of Glen's head now in the Triton's cab. *You could take him if he tried anything*, an attempt at reassurance. But the truth is, Lachlan's never been in a physical scuffle. Not even back in high school.

The next thought freezes him to the spot on the side of the lonesome road. *Maybe this is what happened to Toby?*

Lachlan watches Glen step back from the Triton with a water bottle, not a hammer or tomahawk. 'Git this into ya,' Glen says, chucks it over. 'Might be drizzlin' but she's still a stinker.'

He's already taken his first mouthful, then realises the water could be doped. 'Cheers.' Lachlan tries to smile anyway.

'Where am I takin' ya anyway?'

Lachlan sighs as he locks the Falcon, then wrestles on his backpack and picks up his suitcase. 'Aw, some tiny joint out in absolute bum-fuck nowhere.'

'Plenty'a those out this way.'

'It's called Jasper Cliff.'

Glen grins at him harder. 'Ya havin' me on, youngen?'

'No. Why?'

He laughs. 'S'where I'm headed. Where I live, mate. Bugger me, couldn't have run into a better person to get ya outta this sticky situation.'

All the super-heated tension in his muscles relent, bile relaxing all the way back down his oesophagus, leaving only that slightly acidic tang. 'Finally. A break. That's perfect.'

'But no one goes to the Cliff. Ya wouldn't know we existed if they weren't still printin' us on the maps.' Glen frowns, leans against the Falcon now. 'Don't mean to pry. But can I ask what ya want in the Cliff?'

'I'm looking for my brother. Tobias,' Lachlan says. 'Everyone calls him Toby but.'

A further break; Lachlan watches Glen's face wrinkle with recognition. 'What's ya last name? Didn't catch it.' Then snatches a breath. 'S'not Bowman, is it?'

Lachlan blabbers so fast the words almost merge into a confused whole. 'How-did-you know-that? Do-you-know-Toby? Is-he-still-in-town?'

Glen shakes his head slowly, as if to spare Lachlan any further disappointment. 'Ya just missed him, mate. And by *just* missed him, I mean you're about a month too late.'

'But he was in town?' he asks, not wanting to unclamp himself from this pinprick of hope. 'But you met him? Spoke to him?'

Glen grins. 'We couldn't get rid of him. He shacked up at the pub and wouldn't budge. He was there …' Pauses to consider this and Lachlan squirms with impatience. 'Goin' on eight months, I reckon. Good bloke, ya brother. Real good bloke.'

'And he didn't say anything about where he was going next?'

Glen shakes his head a second time. 'Not to any of us.' He appears to reassess Lachlan now with fresh scrutiny. 'I think I better take ya back to Pippa's. She's the owner of the pub. She'll be able to tell ya heaps more than I can.'

'Thank you so much, Glen.' He's already started hurrying for the tray of the Triton. 'And I'm sorry, by the way.'

Glen follows him over, watches him deposit the pack and case into the ute. 'For what?'

'Uh, the bum-fuck nowhere comment,' then laughs nervously.

Glen watches him, his expression tightening. 'Where you from?'

'Scarborough.'

'Figures,' he says, then shrugs. 'That's okay. We're used to you city-folk treatin' us like a buncha inbred hicks.'

Sounds like it's meant in jest but Glen isn't laughing.

Lachlan experiences a wave of cold, despite the heat out here crammed tight between the ragged acacias. Something unknowable passes across Glen's unreflective eyes; it's like watching a lizard blink, that pale inner eyelid shut and open again in less than a second.

Glen whacks him on the shoulder. 'I'm just rilin' ya, Lachie,' he chuckles, and Lachlan's so relieved to hear that laugh, he almost pisses himself. 'To be fair, most'a us have had a go at a cousin or two at some point in our lives.'

Lachlan chuckles back, trying his best to make it sound genuine. 'Each to their own,' he says, because he's not too sure of what else to say.

'Sometimes, ya just gotta do it.' Laughs. 'Jump in,' Glen says, opening the driver side door. 'Let's get ya back to Pippa's fast as we can.'

Lachlan circles the ute, glancing at his dead Falcon the other side of the road, the mulga tree holding flags of stripped plastic bag in its limbs. Another cold wave of pins and needles scales the length of his body, something deep down telling him to run. But there's no other choice. He has to get in the Triton with the stranger now. He's got to trust someone sometime.

Guesses he'll just have to start by trusting Glen.

From out here on the verandah, she can see the whole sluggish stage of Jasper Cliff.

Their first rain in nearly a year and it's just a shy spittle, really. Despite the doleful sky, it's still hot and muggy, so Pippa leans against the verandah post in a T-shirt and shorts and sips the lemonade she made fresh this morning. Made fresh this morning but not a soul had been through town to try any. Not a single car through, yesterday either. Sometimes she wonders what keeps her hanging on.

The only figure to stir the main street the entire morning emerges now, thongs clapping back against the soles of his heels in a hurry. He's in a singlet in the mizzle, a Bintang one size too big for him. He reaches up to finger the black curls under his threadbare cap and then glances behind him like there might be someone in pursuit.

'Jim!' she sings out. 'Where you going?!'

Parallel with the pub now, but separated by the main street, Shrubb looks up at her. Smiles but then waves a hand and keeps on.

'Come here!' she calls this time.

'Later.' He waves that frantic hand again. 'This arvo maybe.'

'I'm bored. Come talk to me.' She peers down the footpath behind him to see if there is anyone following or if Shrubb has finally lost the plot. 'I made fresh lemonade.'

'Later, later!' He hurries on even quicker now, clownish with how his thongs flap under him. 'Promise!'

She watches him slide away like the last hope of a thirsty man in the desert. No movement from any of the other shops in town. The bakery hasn't been open since September. The shire office only gets busy when the workmen show up once a week to mow the lawns and tinker with the sprinklers, and that is usually on a Monday.

Pippa sculls the last of her drink, relishing the bits of lemon pulp bobbing in the cold glass. Looks to the ghost gum in the road's centre island down past where Shrubb just disappeared. Not even Aunty Belle has made an appearance today.

The town is dying, if this can still be called a town. She's heard the same said for Nullagine. Soon any people left, the desperate hanger-onners, will ship out to the nearest hub – likely Marble Bar – and this will all be left to crumble back into the ground. And maybe that's how it should be. Maybe that's what's meant to happen.

When she first arrived here, it frightened her. This pinprick of human civilisation, rimmed on all sides by jagged chert hills. Her first night in this pub, a solid year and a half before she could afford to buy it off Ol' Mrs Guthrie, she'd never felt so exposed in her life – exposed to the heat and the flies and a feeling of tension hovering over everything, suffusing the very fibre of darkness, the humming earth.

But, eventually, it was the strangeness of Jasper Cliff she fell in love with. How driving into town one forty-three-degree midday, she saw a white goat on the side of the road, right near the Ripon Hills. At first, this didn't draw her attention much at all; she just slowed the car to ensure it didn't freak and trot out in front of the bullbar.

It was only once she was right beside it, she saw the buck was wearing the strangest crown she'd ever seen. Five nodose horns fingered from the cap of its head, straggling away in different directions. Pippa eased on the brakes but by the time she came to a full stop in the bumpy gravel, the white goat had trotted off into the blue-leaved mallees.

She had parked and wandered through the first tier of scrubby trees but the buck was long gone. She couldn't even catch the tailwind of his trotting hooves, his goat-stink. But then the atmosphere of that spot won her over, and although she couldn't see the weird, five-horned goat, she could tell he was somewhere close, watching her, behind a shield of trees.

Jasper Cliff is the strangest place she's ever known, ever could've dreamed of. A place where five-horned goats disappear from roadsides suddenly and you feel the eyes of the country itself staring through the blue-leaved mallees.

Pippa can't stand seeing the town like this, so undignified somehow. How one dog-eared corner of the bakery's patio hangs hopelessly. She would hate to be here when it all finally ends, to witness Jasper Cliff's fall. But it seems inevitable now. She looks down the main street again. Still no cars through today. Might not be any tomorrow either.

But then Pippa looks north and she feels a smile swim across her face like the first mouthful of fresh lemonade. Aunty Belle is sitting under the ghost gum.

She sees Pippa and waves.

Lots of dead eagles on the side of the road. The dead cattle, walloped by road trains, have gone desiccated and deflated, become cow husks, as if they were only ever living skeletons playing fancy dress. Glen sees a dead donkey too.

It's a relief to watch the oppressive cloud cover finally peel back, and a rush of turgid sunlight lap against the back of the Triton. He watches the long shadow of the car stretched upon the road and wonders if somehow the country has been protecting him all this time. As if some agreement has been struck between him and the continent-sized desert, that night he stumbled around euphoric with Muswell's blood on his skin. Surely, someone should've come knocking at his door by now.

When he looks over at his passenger, he watches Lachlan swig down the last of the water. 'How we goin' there?' he asks, catches a glimpse of Muswell sitting in the seat instead, blood oozing between his shattered teeth.

Blinks. No Muswell. All Lachlan again.

'Feeling a bit ordinary if I'm honest.' Lachlan rubs at his pale forehead, sweat gleaming on his fingertips.

'Drink plenty'a water on the drive up?'

'I mean, as much as I could.' Then considers this. 'I guess.'

'Very easy to get dehydrated out here. Ya'll sweat more than ya realise. Trust me.' Glen frowns at him. 'Have to say, ya lookin' a little on the green side.'

Lachlan tries to smile but it wilts quickly. 'Probably just because I thought I'd be stuck out on that road all day. All night too.'

Glen hadn't considered caving in Lachlan's skull yet, not seriously anyway. Not like he had with Muswell. Glen has taken an easy liking to this kid. Well, kid might not be accurate. He looks like he's hit his early thirties already. But there's an innocence about him, a boyish glimmer under the carefully manscaped facial hair. These bloody city folk. Glen's so glad he's not one of them anymore.

Lachlan rubs at his face again, features turning pliable. 'Where are we anyway?'

'These are the Ripon Hills. Not far now.'

Looking at Lachlan fast going the colour of pond scum, he considers if he ever did want that rush again, blood-splattered and sponged up into the dark of the desert, he should probably choose someone who had it coming. Who was deserving. Not dispense some nice kid like Lachlan Bowman just because it was opportune.

The road crescents through a black heap of mulga now and Glen notices the young bloke's started to nudge the console with his knee. Can't help but laugh. 'What do ya think ya doin' to me car there, champ?'

But when he looks over, Lachlan's head is crooked back and both eyes have rolled up in their sockets like veiny, pale bulbs, bubbly spit streaming from the slack left side of his mouth.

'Oh dear shitting Christ!' Glen cries and pulses the Triton's brake.

He's unprepared for the sound, of Lachlan's jolting limbs whacking against the console, the door, the windshield. The ute rocks and bumps around in the gravel until Glen can bring it to a full stop. He's then out of the door and circling around to the passenger side. Through the window for a moment, it looks like a madman's been locked in the cab, gone ballistic in there, violent with mania.

Glen opens the door and feels the rigid, jerking figure fall into his arms. Lucky he's still got a bit of strength in him, all those years labouring at the Westrail workshops in Midland, and catches Lachlan in the cusp of his roughened hands before the kid can crack his head open on the gravel below.

'I dunno what to do,' Glen mutters, trying to find Lachlan's eyes, but they're still hidden in the folds of his skull. 'Tell me what to do, son. Tell me what I gotta do.'

3

After taking a bottle of fresh lemonade down to Aunty Belle, Pippa watches a rift of sunshine breach the overcast, striping the main street. Back inside, she makes for the bar, has just reached for her paperback when the door opens behind her.

Smiles at the way June always takes such care in wiping her feet on the inside mat, streaking the stiff bristles with burgundy. 'What's the goss?' June asks without looking up.

'Oh, you know me, I never speak out of turn.' June's started pouring lemonade without asking. 'Saw Jim this morning. He seemed like he was in a hurry.'

'The police are doing their warrant checks today,' June says with a cheeky grin, aiming for the bar now.

'That's today, is it? Ha. Explains his rush.'

'With the dosh he owes on parkin' fines, he could buy this pub off ya.' She knocks both bony elbows on the bar top and Pippa slides the sweaty glass across. 'You're such a dear.' And swigs the golden liquid. Her eyes rest on the novel under Pippa's hand.

'S'called *Tourmaline.* By Randolph Stow. Ever read it?'

June shakes her head. 'I'm more a Agatha Christie–kinda gal.'

'It's about a little town out in the desert. Slowly dying because they don't have any water.'

'Well, we can't complain about that today, can we?' she says and nods to the open door. The drizzle is still falling despite the fierce sunlight peeking through. 'This's been goin' non-stop since I woke up.'

Pippa huffs and joins June in resting her elbows on the bar. 'So quiet out there today.'

June frowns. 'How's it different to any other, Pip?'

'Dunno. Just feels … *stranger*.' Shrugs. 'Probably the rain. Almost like it doesn't seem right falling out here.' Meets June's eyes. 'How long before Glen's back?'

'Should be today. If we don't see him by this arvo, might have to put the call out to the cops to go lookin' for the silly bugger. His daughter's birthday was the fourteenth so it'd take him a coupla days to get back from the city.'

'Wish he'd keep a bloody mobile so we could at least check up on him.'

'Ya know what men are like. Reckon they can look after themselves.' Flashes her puckish smile. 'Whether they actually can or not is the real question.' She finishes the glass in one last gulp and then lets out a satisfied gurgle. Pippa laughs. 'No one does it better, me love.'

'You're very welcome.'

Now June plays a tattoo on the bar top with her fingers. 'Well, how shall we waste away the day?'

The same as they waste away every day, Pippa supposes. A flash of that first day she took ownership of the hotel cum service station, what lofty ambitions she'd had. For the first week, she got up early and made grilled cheese and prawn nigiri every morning, indulging her love of Japanese food. By that weekend, she hadn't sold a single serve. The truckies and miners sauntered inside after fuelling up, looked at the nigiri and flinched, then asked if she had any Chiko Rolls.

Usually there's Glen and Shrubb here, but she thinks it might be nice for just the girls to hang out today. They wander back out to the verandah and take their designated camp chairs and finally the mizzle has quit. The steaming road leaves them awash in that lovely cooling bitumen smell. Flamboyant galahs make a racket overhead and Aunty Belle is still under the ghost gum down the way, legs folded dexterously.

'Don't need to feel sorry for her,' June says.

Pippa blinks at her, takes her a beat to realise she's talking about the woman under the ghost gum, who sits under that tree every day. Has done as long as Pippa's lived here.

'She wouldn't want ya pity,' June goes on.

'We both know what she wants,' Pippa says. 'What she's waiting for.'

Once the cloud cover has shredded back completely, Jasper Cliff comes to life again. Scarlet, luminescent. An FMG ute trundles into town. Pippa and June watch it slow down beside the petrol tanks.

'Unbelievable,' Pippa says.

'Selfish. What a joker.'

'No thought for anyone else.'

Pippa rouses herself into movement and June shouts at the ute, 'Go get ya bloody fuel from Nullagine! We just sat down!'

Thank God for June. She can always get Pippa laughing.

In retrospect, it must've been so hard for Mum to raise two epileptic kids, him and Toby, especially after their dad said he'd be back an hour late from work, and instead caught a plane over East to shack up with the other, secret, wife and kids he had stashed away in Sydney.

The few times Lachlan had fitted in public had left him more embarrassed than anything, particularly when his body started to seize in the playground in Year 6. He'd half expected to get teased afterwards, but the frightful jerks and the saliva spilling from his mouth appeared to scare the shit out of the kids so much none of them mentioned it.

Grandma had made him the most self-conscious about his epilepsy. Mum said she'd smoked too much dope in the 60s and so was missing a few sheep in the top paddock. His grandmother only witnessed one of his seizures and she reckoned he'd started ranting about something while he was jolting, gargling.

She started in on him and Mum and Toby with all this new-age bullshit about the two boys being percipients of some kind. Reckoned they'd been gifted with the Sight, claimed the boys were having visions of things too far back for them to have known anything about; she'd heard Lachlan raving about one during his fit. She even tried to convince both boys, in private, to stop taking their daily anticonvulsants, because Western medicine surely interfered with these special abilities which the universe had chosen to bestow upon them.

Not sure what's brought on all these inconvenient memories. Because now he's standing on the side of the road and the Triton sits there idling in the mud. When Lachlan pivots slowly, he sees

Glen standing a few metres away in the gravel shoulder. He's staring out at the Ripon Hills, the expression on his tanned face so euphoric it's a little frightening. That look of sheer incautious abandon.

'What are we doing?' Lachlan calls out to him. 'I thought we were going to Jasper Cliff?'

A single tear glissades down the pocked cliffside of Glen's right cheek. And he doesn't answer, doesn't even seem to know Lachlan is close. Can only see the Ripon Hills, in the distance, with devotional eyes.

The black mulga trees all drip with rain, closer to Lachlan, and he sees now they're hanging above a dead Shorthorn bull. Looks like a road train must've cleaned it up because it's such a mess. Fresh too, with the flies sipping on the milkshake of hot blood pooling from the bull's mouth.

The Shorthorn's jaw suddenly pops open and more flies gust from its reeking insides. Despite its mouth extended to the limit, Lachlan can't see much down the dead bull's throat. It's all blackness. Reality appears ruched around the dark crater, disturbed somehow. Matter has failed to fill it in.

Now the jaw rips and tears to get wider, wider, until it's like staring into the depths of a dead volcano. Only darkness within, sheer black, like existence before the Big Bang.

But as Lachlan stares on, he starts to see. The horrific slideshow starts to unfold before his eyes, in a pinprick of light, right at the centre of the void.

And he sees it.

He sees the truth.

He sees what really happened to his little brother.

When Lachlan comes to, he finds Glen kneeling beside him. He has Lachlan's mobile in hand and hangs back as if afraid getting too close might set Lachlan off fitting again.

'Thank fuck,' he says. 'I was about to try call the ambos but I don't know the code on your little gadget here.'

'Gadget?' he mutters and blinks his muzzy eyes, head throbbing. The sky seems to heave closer as if pregnant with rain. 'It's a phone, Glen.'

'Infernal things.' When Lachlan tries to sit up, Glen gently places a hand on his shoulder. 'Tell me what the code is and I'll call for the ambos.'

'No need,' Lachlan tells him, shoving Glen's hand away a bit harder than he meant to. 'I'm epileptic.'

'Oh shit,' Glen says now, straightens and hands the phone back nonchalantly. 'Are ya on some kinda medication for that?'

'Yeah, it's okay. Still happens sometimes. It's rare but it happens.' Once back on his feet, Lachlan falls against the side of the Triton, imprinting the windshield with one sweat-damp palm to hold himself up. 'I am really bloody thirsty. Never felt so thirsty.'

Glen hurries around to the back door with the empty water bottle and starts filling it again from the tank.

'Haven't had a seizure in like five years, fuck,' Lachlan tells the watching spinifex hills and notices how they appear too bright, everything just a little too lucid now. Reality keeps slapping him in the face like cold breakers off the sea.

'Git this into ya.' Glen hands back the water bottle.

Lachlan sculls it in one go.

'I really would like to call the ambos. Wouldn't feel right otherwise.'

But Lachlan shakes his head, that familiar embarrassment of being treated like an invalid; he even feels his cheeks go hot to hear this. Always a bit vague after coming to, but this is something new. Notices how some sunlight has pierced the cloud cover above them, a beam of cherry light cometing, the consistency of wine.

'Just need to sit down,' he mumbles.

Swift as some swanky hotel attendant, Glen opens the passenger side door and says, 'Here. Jump in. You're right, you're all good now.'

Lachlan slumps into the seat, lets the empty bottle fall between his legs. Still the hot beam of light shafts through the Triton.

Then Glen gets in behind the wheel. 'You're okay, Lachie. We're almost there anyway, mate. If ya won't let me call the ambos, I can get Pip to give ya a once over. Probly for the best anyhow, the nearest nursing station's in Marble Bar. It'd take them a while to get out here.'

It's only when that febrile light carves out the strange topography of Glen's weathered face that Lachlan remembers the vision he had when he was fitting. He can feel himself fading. He tries to reach for the door handle but he's so groggy.

'Where are we going?' Lachlan mumbles, spit bubbling slightly in both corners of his mouth. 'Where are you taking me, Glen?'

'The Cliff, remember?' he tells Lachlan, frowning.

Lachlan tries to remember what he saw when the dead bull's mouth slowly yawed open. But it's like trying to remember a dream the morning after, always slipping from his grip, just when he thinks he has a grasp on the bloody thing.

Glen turns to look at him, still confused. 'We're goin' to Jasper Cliff, aren't we?'

June heads inside to ring up the till after Pippa fills the mining ute's tank; it's a service no one else in the East Pilbara provides. A small service which, she's always hoped, makes her stand out from the rest of the roadhouses this way; ninety-nine percent are self-serve or even unmanned tanks. Once the two men – decked out in company-issue long-sleeve tops and pants despite the raging heat – have taken off again, Pippa and June retake their seats. Watch the uneventful main street.

Pippa tries to recall how many days they've done this the past year. Probably every day, or just about. Even when Toby was still here. Sometimes the days beyond the pub's verandah are simply too hot to endure for longer than an hour at a time. So it's easier just to laze around in the shade and talk shit and do nothing much at all. Conserve energy.

'Saw that dingo again,' June tells her, breaking the sticky weight of silence.

'This the female?'

'Yeah, out on Marble Bar–Ripon Hills Road. I honestly can't figure out how she's still alive. I saw her six months ago in almost the exact same spot and she was all bones. Twiggy. This time all her hair had this diseased look to it.'

'Like mange?'

June nods. 'She must be livin' off the roadkill. Must know

where there's some water nearby. Only way I can figure she's still alive. Any other dog woulda laid down under a bloodwood and carked it by now.'

'And she was alone?' Pippa hears herself ask this and experiences a depressing rush of gloom, trying to push the thought of Toby away.

'Probly too sick for the pack to stick around and look after her.' June shrugs like this is completely understandable. 'So they left her behind.'

Pippa makes a note to ask June exactly where she saw the sickly dingo and she'll drive out that way later tonight after she's shut the pub. She can take one of the chuck steaks out of the fridge and leave it in the same spot. Even if she doesn't see the dingo, she'd like to know she might've helped in some way.

But then she recalls the five-horned goat. Only the day after she spotted that freakish buck, she'd returned to the same patch of road, weirdly drawn back to it, more by the heady feeling of being watched in the blue-leaved mallees. She'd waited until five in the evening and yet the lateness of day had done little to stifle the rageful heat. She picked through the mallees, hoping she'd feel those all-seeing eyes on her again.

The locals had warned her that sometimes domestic dogs from town took off to join the packs of dingoes in the Ripon Hills, having undergone some unknowable transformation to be considered one of the crew. This had surely been one such domestic, now gone frightfully feral.

The animal's enormous back struggled against a heifer's carcass in the gravel and when it did finally emerge from the cow's guts, it looked like the head of sea lion yanked itself from an ocean of blood. A Bernese mountain dog. Usually so doted upon, host to a shiny, shampooed coat, this thing was all prickles and grass seeds and snags. Surely too heavy, too dark a colour, to survive in this country; she guessed its adoptive pack must've been taking good care of it.

Pippa had turned and bolted out of the hakea scrub, wrenched the car door open and thrashed back inside. Once safe inside the cab, she looked through the window and saw the mountain dog blinking out the fresh heifer blood, sniffing curiously around her RAV4. The dog was about half the size of the car. She'd escaped in a hurry but the encounter had left her trembling with bright adrenaline, staring out at the Ripon Hills with a refreshed sense of terrible wonder.

It was on the same stretch of road June saw the sickly dingo. She thinks twice about taking a steak out there.

'Here's the silly bugger now,' June says, nodding at the far end of the main street.

Pippa looks up, recognises Glen's dirty Triton. This time it's fully caked in hardening mud. 'He's going to sleep like a bloody baby after doing that trip from Perth in two days straight.'

June stands from her chair, waves. Then the wave quickly flips into the rude finger.

The ute squeals a little on the cracked tarmac, pulling up in front of the pub.

'Hoon,' June says.

Once the Triton's stopped and hangs there idling, Pippa can see there's someone in Glen's passenger seat; for a split second she suspects he's brought his daughter all the way back from the city. She looks at the stranger, who appears to be asleep or close to it, and can't help but think he looks very much like Toby.

Just your eyes seeing what they want to see, Pippa reminds herself. *It's alright to let yourself miss him.* Clenches her teeth. *Or hate him, more like it.*

She only realises something's wrong when she watches Glen rush from around his side of the car to the passenger side; she's never seen Glen move so fast. He calls over the top of the muddy bonnet. 'Might need a hand here. This young bloke's had a bit of a rough trot.'

Both Pippa and June are by the ute's side in a heartbeat. They reach to lend a helping hand but the man shakes his head. 'I'm okay, really,' the stranger says. 'Every'shhing's fine.'

He doesn't look fine, though. Looks like he hasn't trained for a marathon but has tried to run it anyway, legs limp and face slack, and he makes a slurry of everything he says. 'I'm absholutely sh'fine.'

Meeting his eyes now, much closer, Pippa gets pins and needles head to toe. He looks a lot like Toby. Just much less scruffy and maybe a few years older.

But Toby's gone.

She shakes her head to clear the cobwebs away. 'Uh, come inside. It's heaps cooler.'

Glen reaches in to help the stranger but this time he shakes his hands frantically, like they're a pack of over-friendly dogs all licking and slobbering and panting at him. Pippa stands back with June and Glen and watches him stumble from the ute. He makes it onto the verandah, weaving only a little, wrestling with sea legs. Pippa and Glen look at each other before following him in.

'Ask him who he is,' Glen says, raising his eyebrows. 'Why he's here.'

When the three of them step into the pub, the stranger has found one of the stools at the bar and is resting his forehead against the beer mat. He peers up at himself in the long, slightly grubby, mirror which stretches just below the empty liquor shelves. June slips furtively over to the fridge, pours a glass of homemade lemonade. The stranger doesn't say thank you, just swigs the glass empty.

'So fucken hot here,' he says. 'I've never known it so hot.'

'Gunna push forty-three today,' June tells him.

Glen takes the seat next to the young man. 'How are ya feelin' now? Should ya take some of that medication you're on?'

Shakes his head. 'Doesn't work like that.'

'What happened?' Pippa asks, joining June on the other side of the bar now, the side she'd stand if she sold grog in here anymore.

He goes to answer but Glen cuts in, 'He had a fit.'

'Shit,' says June.

He glances at Glen peevishly. When he speaks next, he forces each word out deliberately and without slurring, as if to avoid any further shame. 'I'm epileptic. It's fine. Lived with it my whole life.' Now he's fully raised his head and looked around at the three of them, he blushes hard; Pippa's never seen someone so embarrassed. 'I'm *fine*. Truthfully.'

'Well, that's the main thing anyway.' Glen thumps him on the back, then nods across the bar top. 'This is Pip, who I was tellin' ya about. She owns the pub. And this is June.'

He smiles shyly at them both. 'Lachlan.'

'Tell 'em ya last name.'

Lachlan scowls at him, then addresses Pippa and June directly. 'I'm looking for my little brother, Toby. Glen says he was staying here for a while.'

Pippa's always thought the pub was too dark, ever since she'd bought it off Mrs Guthrie. She's done her best to encourage an assault of natural light in here but it's almost like the walls are actively trying to repel it. She can't imagine it getting any darker, but it does now. The room or the inside of her chest cloaked by grim shadow.

'Yeah,' she says. 'He was.'

Now Pippa notices June and Glen are staring at her with the worst expressions of all – pity. It's her turn to be embarrassed.

June saves her, turning to Lachlan. 'He was here like eight, nine months, yeah. Real nice bloke, your brother. It was a pleasure to have him around.'

But Lachlan must see something in Pippa's face, some glistening hope, because he won't break eye contact now. 'And he didn't say a word about where he was going next?'

Pippa examines a sticky Coke stain on the bar she must've missed the last time she ran the tea towel over it. 'No, he didn't. We woke up one morning and he was gone. No word, no letter, no text. Nothing.'

Lachlan sighs. 'That's what's got me freaked. Tobes was flighty as all hell. Always looking forward to hitching a ride along to whatever bright idea he was working on next. But he always called me and Mum. Always kept us up to date. Didn't always give us all the details, but always gave us a location.'

'He call you from here?' Glen asks. 'From the Cliff?'

Lachlan nods. 'Heaps of times. Like I said, he was cagey about what exactly he was doing here, but he was moving around a lot. Said he was working real dreggy jobs for a bit. Started in Cue. Worked in the IGA there. Then when he had enough money, he went up to Marble Bar, Nullagine. Ended up here.' He looks at Pippa again, wondering. 'I did think it was weird he'd stayed here so long.' Looks at Glen. 'Never sounded like there was ever really much here.'

Glen shakes his head. 'There ya go slaggin' off us country folk again.'

'He never mentioned …' Pippa starts, then once she hears the choke in her voice, she clears it and starts again. 'He never mentioned you or your mum.'

'He could be like that,' Lachlan tells her, and her directly, not including June or Glen. 'Quiet. Too quiet, I suppose. He was working on a novel, you know? That's why he came up this way. Mum always used to take us on holidays up north. He always loved the mulga, the heat. He's done pretty well with his writing. He's had short stories published.' Lachlan lowers his head then, either because Pippa and June and Glen have blank faces upon hearing that, or because he is so exhausted. 'I'm so fucken freaked out now.'

'Ya just tired,' Glen tells him. 'Ya need sleep.' Then turns to June. 'Drove eight hours today.'

'About the same as you then,' June responds.

'His car's back on Munjina–Roy Hill Road.'

'Are ya with RAC?' June asks.

Glen answers, 'The motor's cooked. It'll be a tow job.'

'Shit me. Ya really are havin' a shit of a day, aren't ya?'

Pippa leans a little towards him, but not too close with the strange way the planes of his face pay some similitude to Toby's. 'Don't worry about any of that now,' she says. 'You can have one of the rooms here for the night. Get a good night's sleep and we can start sorting everything out in the morning.'

As if he hasn't heard any of this, or been reassured at all, he looks at Pippa again. 'When was the last time you saw him?'

Pippa glances at Glen and June. 'Um, October seventeenth. He was here October seventeenth. Then him and his car and all his stuff was gone the next morning when I woke up.'

Lachlan studies her a long time. 'You two were together.' Not a question.

Pains her to nod, slowly.

'Why didn't you call me? Someone?'

'Like I said, Toby didn't mention he had any family. Not once. I'm sure I even asked him.' She looks between Glen and June again, as if desperate to be backed up. 'And I didn't report him missing because …' When she meets Lachlan's eyes again, she hates herself even more than usual; the way he's hanging on every word. 'We had an argument the night before. Nothing crazy. But let's just say, I wasn't completely bewildered the next morning when I woke up and he was gone.'

'Well, that's the first thing I'm going to do now,' he says a little bitterly, as if laying the blame firmly at her feet. 'Report him missing.' He slides off his stool, but then snakes to the ground lifeless as a crash test dummy.

June hurries around the side of the bar to help Glen drag the newcomer back to his feet. Pippa wonders if she should've done the same but can barely move staring at his face again. It's a bit like Toby's but not quite enough, like a bad disguise. A Toby-phantasm.

'I'm okay, I'm okay,' Lachlan has started to babble awkwardly again.

'Ya can call the cops from that newfangled phone ya got, but ya can do it in bed. We gotta get ya off ya feet.'

June leads the way down the hall to open up the nearest guest-room. Glen doesn't so much help Lachlan but hangs just behind him with both hands open, like he can reach out and steady him if he keels over again.

But then Lachlan stops, some colour filling his cheeks again, like when he got embarrassed. 'Were you in love?'

It's an odd question, and thankfully Glen tells him not to worry about all that now and rushes him on into the hall. Pippa can't believe the plunging sense of relief, the feeling of icy water trickling through all her overheated muscles, to have Lachlan gone from sight. She rests both hands against the bar top in a feigned attempt to hold herself upright.

She turns to see her reflection in the long mirror behind the bar, the sweat in a greasy slick across the shiny crown of her brow. She backhands it away. She breathes and her stomach tumbles once or twice over itself. The fear turns glassy in her eyes.

What if he's right? Pippa thinks. *What if you've been wrong this entire time? And Toby didn't take off because of the argument? Anything could've happened to him. He's been gone for a month already. A whole bloody month.*

She watches June return, or her backward mirror image. 'Come out the front,' June says.

Pippa follows her to the verandah and they take their chairs again, though now Pippa bothers her bottom lip with her front teeth. Then chews too hard and hisses. 'I didn't think,' she says.

'I know, bub. But none of us did. We all knew Tobes, and I can honestly say I never thought that maybe somethin' bad had happened to him.' June looks over Jasper Cliff, all its sharp contours softening under the ruby light. 'Maybe we should've? This town bein' this town. This place this place. I guess it was his car gone that made me think it was his own choice.' Glances over. 'And …'

'Us arguing the night before.'

June sighs. 'It was a rowdy one. I could hear it from my joint down the way.'

'It was that loud? Christ. You never told me that.' Pippa keels forward and cups her face in her hands. 'Oh God, June. What if something really awful's happened to him?'

'Early days yet, love. Early days.' She feels June's hand rest in the middle of her back. 'Oi. Look at me.'

She does. June's wrinkled expression, steadfast as bedrock, hair wild like gulfweed. 'He'll be okay. Gotta think positive.'

Pippa squeezes her hand. 'Shit, I didn't think how all this talk might be affecting you. I'm sorry. Are you alright?'

'I'm just dandy, love. I'm sure it's exactly what ya were thinkin'. Things heated up too much between you and Tobes and he took off like a shot. Ya know what men are like. Gettin' them to commit's like tryin' to get blood outta a stone.'

Pippa breathes. 'And Jim. At least Jim's not here to hear any of this.'

'Nup, he's down there with Belle.' June nods.

When Pippa looks down the main street, a volley of galahs streams overhead, shrieking. Under the ghost gum, Shrubb and Aunty Belle are sitting together. Shrubb's talking, picking out handfuls of lawn with a restive kind of anxiety, and Aunty Belle is nodding away, patiently listening to whatever he's saying.

'We're all stronger than ya think, bub,' June tells her, pats her on the back and then settles snugly into her chair. 'And so's Toby. I think young Lachie in there is just panicked, that's all. And it's understandable.'

Pippa glares down the main street for some time, realising eventually she's looking past Shrubb and Aunty Belle and is fixated on the lower foothills of the Barite Range hemming in this poor excuse for a town. The magnitude of those hills, and Toby could be somewhere out in all that. Or shacked up with a younger girl in a backpacker's hostel somewhere. Despite how she feels for the bastard, she thinks she'd prefer the latter. At least she'd know he was still alive. Even if he turned out to be a womanising arsehole, no better than the rest of them. At least then she could simply hate him, rather than feel scared to death for him.

Shrubb finishes talking to Belle now and starts down the footpath towards the pub, dishevelled and with thongs flapping. A huge, silly smile on his face because he's missed all the excitement of Toby's older brother showing up.

The most excitement they've had in a long time.

Lachlan's conked out already, face turned to the wall, so Glen can only see the back of his head. Muswell had a skull like cast iron. A couple of times when Glen swung that star picket, it even made a slight twanging sound upon connecting with the little bugger's face. His nose made a wetter, cracking noise as the cartilage broke open and he spat out blobs of gore.

Weird to remember that now, after what happened today. Something about the juxtaposition unnerves him. As Lachlan fitted in the gravel, Glen had dropped to his knees, grimacing at how painful his right one was, accelerator-side – the fang-wounds in his calf throbbing with terrible joy – and slid both hands under the back of Lachlan's head. Otherwise, with how he jerked and spasmed, it would've been way too easy for the young bloke to crack his skull open on the sharp rocks.

It felt kind of good actually, to be saving Lachlan from harm, as his eyes bobbed around like shelled eggs and the spit streamed over his clacking teeth – to hold something as fragile as a human head in his hands and not break it.

Felt good, sure – and Glen's oddly proud of himself for it – but it couldn't compare to the night after he dispatched Muswell. The heave of the desert occupying what was left of the world beyond him.

Simply nothing could compare to that.

4

Lachlan wakes again and this time there's no dream or premonition to rouse him. Sits up in the stuffy hotel bed, this mattress and pillows and sheets untouched by another human body for so long. Usually, hotel beds retain the smell of strangers; no amount of laundry liquid can dispel it.

He's surprised to pick the brittle crust from his eyes and see the room has expanded pale with moonlight, flaring through the window above his head. At first, he's completely unanchored. Moving from place to place, driving from home to Cue, following the traces Toby left behind. Then up to the Auski Roadhouse. Then the fucker of a car breaking down, and Glen, the seizure, and now Jasper Cliff.

More and more strange faces, the kindness of these strangers, but still no Toby.

He sees now he's kicked the sheets from his legs in sleep and they lie in a hillock on the floor. There's a density to the air, the heat jammed into every tight space, like he's breathing kettle steam. Lachlan sidesteps the sheets, goes out into the darkened bar and when he looks to the open door, he can see someone standing outside. A turned back, all profile.

That vision he had of Glen earlier, the sole tear on his cheek. Can't tell now why he'd felt any trepidation around the old bloke. Seems silly. After all, Lachlan would be waking up on the side of that lonely road right now if it wasn't for Glen. Weirdly, he can even recall how the man's gentle hands had cupped his head, cradling his skull careful as holding a crystal ball.

'How are you feeling?' Pippa asks as he steps out the open door to join her. She doesn't turn, can just sense him near.

Lachlan takes the opportunity to assess her unseen. She isn't exactly Toby's type; he usually goes after hippie chicks. Full-tilt vegans who chain themselves to concrete blocks outside the Rio Tinto building in Perth. Pippa doesn't fit. She's scrawny and very tall and sombre. That deathly English pale, even ghoulish in this light.

'Tons better. Thanks so much.'

The main street swells with argent moonlight. Just about every surface adorned with corrugated iron so the walls and rooftops ripple like an interconnected chain of waterholes and ponds.

'Can't sleep?' Lachlan asks her, leaning against the verandah post, but ensuring he's maintaining a healthy distance. He's not Toby, can't promise her anything in that respect.

She gives him a faint smile. 'Problem I'm having lately.'

'About earlier, that was bloody rude. Asking about you and Tobes. Asking if you two were a thing.' Rubs at his face and lets out a high-pitched laugh. 'He's my brother but that's none of my business.'

'It didn't bother me,' she says, and Lachlan notices she's staring down the street at a ghost gum. The tree has soaked up the colour of the moon, its light some magic liquor poured into a wizened pipe glass. It appears as if she's looking for something under that night-light tree but there's just bare lawn below its leaves.

'Still. I want to apologise.' He notices a shadow flick past, then again. Must be a bat swooping for bugs. 'June woke me up not long after I conked out. Did she tell you?'

Pippa nods. 'She's good like that, our June.'

'I called Mum. She said she'd get onto the police, file a missing person report. She's completely losing it, as you can imagine. I feel shithouse. Should be there with her, you know? She told me not to worry about it, but I could hear it in her voice. How scared she is.' He shrugs. 'But it's not like I can do anything about it. Especially considering my car might be out of commission for a while. And I can't get Vodafone reception out here.'

Pippa turns to looks at him again. 'You're welcome to stay here as long as you need.' Then a second smile, this one with some real feeling in it. 'You're actually my first guest in over a year. Excluding Toby.'

His breath sounds harried, and he wonders if Pippa can hear it as loud as he can. 'He really didn't say anything? About what he was doing? Where he might've been going?'

The bat glides just centimetres in front of her face; she mustn't have noticed because she doesn't flinch. 'I honestly never thought, not once, that he could've got himself into any kind of trouble. If I had, the cops would've heard about it long before now. And you and your mum.'

When he turns back, Pippa is watching him again. Okay, maybe he can see what drew Toby to her now. The moonlight glows in her teal eyes. And right now, she appears resolute, unmovable, like a granite isle at sea. Hair glossy where it's cropped around her face, and she looks like a Hollywood starlet from the Golden Age.

'The argument I mentioned.'

'You don't have to tell me.'

'I want to. Just in case it turns out to be important,' she says. 'It was about kids. I always wanted them, and he didn't. I guess things had moved pretty quickly between us and I thought it was time we had the conversation. Or at least brought it up with him. Turned out it was something he'd never even considered. Had no interest in whatsoever. I guess that surprised me a little. And we got into it from there.'

Lachlan nods, as if he understands this. 'Our father walked out on us when we were kids. Toby was still little, but old enough to remember it all. Found out later Dad had a second family stashed away over in Sydney. Guess that's what all those long business trips were really for, eh?'

He forces himself to chuckle but it sounds like rocks flung up against ripple iron. 'I think it definitely made me think differently about fatherhood. Not to take that responsibility lightly, you know? I'm just guessing – because we never really discussed it – but maybe it was the same for Tobes?'

She looks back at the cool light lacquering the main street. 'Sounds like it would've played a part. But there was the other stuff too. That obsessive side of him. Too busy hunting after something that might not even be real. A figment of his imagination which almost occupied as much room in his head as I did maybe.'

Lachlan frowns. 'Hunting? After what?'

'The Rift.'

He's never heard this before, and yet Lachlan reels, heady with moonlight or still recovering from his seizure – or somehow put under the magic of whatever his little brother was pursuing. 'The what?'

'I'll tell you about it tomorrow.' Pippa unsticks herself from the verandah post, looks back at the doorway. 'You should get some more rest.'

With that, she leaves him alone. Just him and Jasper Cliff. He glances back down at the gleaming ghost gum but there's no one sitting underneath. Not entirely sure why he was expecting there to be.

The Rift, he thinks, getting a wonderful sprawl of goosebumps with it.

No wonder his little brother loved this town; this place is a mystery. And Toby always liked a good mystery.

When Pippa steps back into her bedroom, she lingers above the bed and finds her hearing has amplified tenfold. She's listening for the sound of Lachlan returning to his room. But there's no footsteps; he must've decided to stay out in the moonlight a bit longer.

It's a little unsettling to have someone else sleeping in the pub after so long. A sort-of-Toby-lookalike but not Toby. Surreal as the strange angle of moonlight coming in through the window above the bed she and Toby had shared for so long. It's like the axis on which Jasper Cliff has always turned has skewed ever so slightly – if only a millimetre – the moment Glen returned to town with Lachlan in the passenger seat.

Pippa strips off her sweat-damp singlet, then her shorts, and she's about to thump onto the mattress in nothing but her undies when she sees that she left *Tourmaline* on her bed earlier. This late in the dark, this exhausted, she almost swipes it angrily to the floor.

Toby had given it to her the first day they met. As he slid it across the top of the bar with that big smile on his face, Pippa watched the blonde hairs on her arm stand on end, her skin freckling with slowly emerging Braille. He couldn't have known, couldn't have had any possible idea, about what happened at The Glenmore. She had to keep reminding herself of that.

When she'd first landed in Sydney, enduring the hellish flight across the curvature of the globe from London, she'd met a man very much like Toby at The Glenmore in The Rocks. They hit it off quickly once Pippa realised they were both big readers, and he insisted she dive headfirst into the great female authors this nation had to offer, the likes of Elizabeth Harrower and Alexis Wright.

They'd caught up for coffee a few times overlooking the harbour when he showed up to The Glenmore with a copy of *Picnic at Hanging Rock* by Joan Lindsay. He'd just bought it from a bookshop on King Street and she can still remember how her stomach flopped over on itself with excitement when she ran a thumb across the pages and smelt its newly minted bookness.

Later that night, they went back to her room on the second storey of The Glenmore. She hadn't had sex for two years, not since her final year of uni, so she was a little nervous while he was assured, unwavering. Brushed her from ear to collarbone with his lips. Whispered delicately to her but she could hear in his excited breath how hurried he was.

When he pushed inside, she was unprepared for the pain.

Didn't make much sense to her as she was certain she was already in love with him, though they'd only known each other a fortnight. Her body just wasn't receptive in the same way her mind was. It happens, she told herself.

The problem was he ploughed on anyway, though he could see her grimacing in pain, hissing every time he tried to lurch deeper inside. 'I'm sorry,' she'd whispered. 'We have to stop. Something – something's not right.'

She saw the shift in his eyes then, how they went from gentle, if a little greedy, to mean blackness. Even his irises changed colour, a shark smelling seal blood in the water.

'You can't back out now, I've already started,' he told her so calmly her heart went cold. 'If you're not into it, you're just going to have to suck it up and wait till I'm done.'

While the urge to shove him and squirm free of his awful, sweaty weight, was unbearable, Pippa could only feel her muscles lock her into place, betraying her, clamping her to the mattress. And yet she held those hungry eyes. 'Get off me. Right now.'

'Stop talking.' This time an instruction. 'Because you're not leaving until I've finished. Got it?'

Without thinking, Pippa realised she'd rested her thumb under his right eye. She had no idea where this surplus of strength had come from, as if it had always been there, indefatigable – some animal engine guttering within.

When she jammed her thumb in, she was half expecting his eyeball to pop like a cork from its socket. The sensation was so disquieting she shrieked just as loudly as he did when he floundered off her and sprawled across the floor.

In the terrible silence which followed, she watched him wiping at the blood under his right eye, in the raw and out of breath and beaded with sweat. She hadn't even come close to popping the eyeball out; she saw now she'd basically just given him a scratch. He stood only a moment longer, doing the sum in his head, deciding whether it was worth trying to attack her again, before he got dressed without a word and went back out. He didn't even slam the door behind him.

She stayed caught in the trap of bedding, listening to the creak of his footsteps going down the stairs, needing to be sure he was gone.

Pippa locked the hotel door and took that copy of *Picnic at Hanging Rock* and opened the window and lobbed it out into the dirty alley below.

She flumps into bed now and looks at *Tourmaline*. She'd never told Toby that story, didn't want to soil their moments together between these very walls. She'd been scared shitless of men for a long time after what happened to her at The Glenmore, until the day that ragged stranger showed up on her doorstep.

At first, he'd only frightened her further with how he smiled at her. How he handed her *Tourmaline*, and it was anything but brand new. Scored here and there and smudged with red-dirt thumbprints. She'd hidden the novel under the bar, not wanting to touch it.

She'd completely forgotten about it until the day after Toby left, when she found it again. As she placed the book gently on top of the bar and turned the first page, she drew in a deep breath and started to read.

Catches herself in a hard swallow as the pub's front door closes. She listens to Toby's older brother return to his room but now her body's firing with adrenaline, pulse tapping insistently under her jaw. The wooden stairs in The Glenmore still creaking behind her racing heart. Shouldn't let herself feel like this. It's been so long since she was afraid.

She picks up the book and decides to read for a bit. Then she might actually fall asleep. But somehow she doubts it, not as her pale skin continues to prickle.

When Lachlan tiptoes out of the pub, the heat is like some other element suffusing the very air out here. Human beings shouldn't be able to withstand it, shouldn't be able to exist in country like this.

Six o'clock in the morning and the sweat's already darkened his shirt and shorts in bands around his chest and waist. He's breathless by the time he reaches the deli alongside the ghost gum in the centre nature strip of the main street. A flapping paper catches his eye, halts him in his hunt for a payphone.

The front wall of the dingy store is covered with missing persons posters. There's a dry click in Lachlan's throat as he swallows. Weirdly, he half expects to see his little brother's face among them but that's not possible as mum only made the report with the police last night. The cops must've put these pictures up a long time ago, with how frayed and ragged around the edges they are. And when he looks closer, most of these strangers have been missing as long as five years. Some only six months ago. He swerves away again before the dread can climb any higher inside his chest.

The payphone bobs down the other end of the footpath like an unmanned tinny at sea. When he checked his mobile again this morning, he remembered there was no reception. Only Telstra in backwater joints like this. June had let him borrow her dodgy old Nokia yesterday while he lounged in bed.

He reaches the phone box the other side of the deli and notices a boy, must only be eight or nine years old, sitting in a wrecked RAV4; the first person he's seen in town this morning. The four-wheel drive is parked in the middle of a block choking on yellow grass. The car is missing every door and its engine and its windscreens. The boy sits wordlessly in the driver's seat with the assorted car junk all about – some timeless creature untouched by the passing of a millennium – the RAV4 rapidly falling apart around him.

Lachlan tries three towing services in the nearest regional city on the coast, two-and-a-half hours drive away, and none will send a truck out as far as Jasper Cliff. One lady even asks, 'Jasper *what*? Where the hell is that?'

'Shit shit shit,' he chants. He tries RAC but they won't go further than fifty kilometres from any regional centre. He even tries his luck with a couple of mechanics.

'Shit!' he cries and breaks the receiver against the cubicle.

Stillness after, and Lachlan peers down at the black pieces of plastic around his feet, the spaghetti of wires spewing from the broken receiver. He's never done anything like this in his life, lost it so easily, and so publicly.

When he looks back to the spare block, the boy is standing beside what remains of the car, not afraid but watching on curiously. Lachlan winces at him. 'Sorry, mate.'

'Ya know there's only one'a them in town, right?' a man asks from beside the payphone.

Lachlan starts, didn't even hear the stranger approach. He grimaces a little to look at the man's greasy dark curls trying to wriggle free from under his ragged cap. The stranger's face droops as if he hasn't had enough sleep and yellowed toenails flare when he wiggles his hairy feet in thongs.

Finally, what he just said sinks in and Lachlan looks at the broken phone. 'Seriously?'

'Yeah, that's why we try not fuck the thing up, mate.' He waves at the boy in the spare block too now. 'Tryin' to get Telstra out here's like tryin' to get a bitch to lay kittens.'

Lachlan lets the shattered receiver dangle. 'I can't believe this.' He looks back at the totalled RAV4 but the kid has turned his back and is walking away.

'That was Pip's car. Chucked the shits last year. She tried to sell it for parts but no one'd come out from the coast to collect it.' The man plumbs both hands into the pockets of his footy shorts. 'You Toby's big bro? Glen told me 'bout ya yesterday. Ya car cracked a tanty, eh?'

'Yeah, and no one will come out this far to tow the useless thing.'

The man sniffs, looks around. Through the spare block with the wrecked RAV4, they can see the further reaches of Jasper Cliff. Not much more of it. What looks like a police station and a sprinkling of houses. 'I'll ask around for ya,' he says. 'Not makin' any promises. But someone round here might be able to help out.'

'That'd be great,' Lachlan grumbles, before realising he sounds ungrateful. Then lifts his pitch. 'Thanks. Didn't catch your name.'

'Jim. But most round here call me Shrubb. Only Pip really calls me Jim.'

'Lachlan.'

'I'm sorry to hear ya haven't seen Tobes. He was a nice bloke, ya brother. We had some good times while he was holed-up here.' Shrubb tries his hardest not to look down at the missing persons papers flapping on the front of the deli, but by trying not to look, Lachlan can tell what he's thinking. 'I'm sure he'll be just fine. I've half expected him to come flyin' back into town one'a these days. Grovellin' at Pippa's feet.'

'We can only hope,' Lachlan's voice returns to a grumble. 'That would be the best-case scenario.'

'I just assumed he went lookin' for the Rift somewhere else,' Shrubb adds, now watching the boy wander away through a shock of river red gums.

The Rift. The same thing Pippa mentioned last night.

'What is this Rift thing? Is it like a gorge or something?'

Shrubb twitches, as if realising he's spoken out of turn. 'Think ya better ask Pip about all that. Not really me forte.'

He evaluates Lachlan closer, empathy nearly breaking the contours on his face. 'It's somethin' Toby reckons he saw, that's all. It's a bit of a tall tale the old blokes used to spin round here. Toby reckons he saw somethin' like it, but down in Cue. Then he heard there were stories of a similar thing up here.' He removes one hand from his pocket and plays with his dark goatee, specks of grey in it. 'Bit of a dreamer, ya brother.'

Lachlan looks at the payphone. 'Well, I've fucked this now,' he says. 'Can I borrow your phone?'

'Don't have one.'

Lachlan scowls at him.

'Can live quite comfortably in a place like the Cliff without a phone, mate.'

'Fuck my life.'

'I'm goin' up to Pip's. Comin'? She'll let ya use the pub phone.'

'Didn't want to bother her. She's already helped me out heaps.'

He shrugs. 'Beggars can't be choosers.'

After glancing back at the deli one last time, the flapping faces of the lost, Lachlan focuses on the footpath, tries to clear his head. This time, he stays on the right side of the main street, slowing down in order to match Shrubb's pace. Past a Shire Works office and a butchery and an unmanned community resource centre. He wonders if they'll open at nine o'clock, if at all.

Swollen with yolky morning light, the locus of the town looms ahead, right across from Pippa's pub. It's some kind of memorial. When Lachlan stops and squints, he sees lines and lines of plaques for the first prospectors who arrived in Jasper Cliff, gave it a name, started erecting all this corrugated iron. The plaques are attached to a white brick wall. Weirdly, each has a name, year of death and cause of death.

'This is a bit morbid, isn't it?' Lachlan asks.

Shrubb looks on. 'The historical society set it up a few years back. A way of showin' visitors just how tough life was back in the day.' He looks up and down the main street. 'Not that there are many visitors to read about that.'

Caley, Jonathon. Died 1887. Fell down a mineshaft.

Coppin, Daniel. Died 1883. Speared by Nyamal warriors.

Cooper, Reginald. Died 1899. Gunshot wound to the face, self-inflicted.

'Hard life back then,' Shrubb adds.

As Lachlan looks from dull plaque to plaque, reading these feels like stealing the names of ghosts. And Shrubb's right. The least atrocious cause of death Lachlan can find is *Died of liver failure* – the publican of all people.

Shrubb's still standing right next to him, so he can't tell whose shadow he can see tumbling in the corner of his eye. An amalgam of the names, souls merged into some penumbral mass and roiling towards him. He catches his breath and looks up and down the street, then up into the sky. Only town and sky and road.

Shrubb looks just as freaked. 'Hell's the matter?'

Lachlan tastes his bad breath. Looking up at the ghost gum, he sees there's a child's bicycle at least three metres up in the tree, a branch hanging onto it by the spokes. Wonders how that got up there, deposited by flood or cyclone?

'You didn't feel that?' Lachlan asks.

'It's just this place,' Shrubb says, and nods at the plaque. 'All the death that made this town.' He turns to lead Lachlan away. 'Carn. Let's get some caffeine in ya.'

Lachlan allows himself to look back one last time at the memorial. The closest plaque reads: *Shrubb, Leonard. Died 1901. Fell off his horse and broke his neck.*

He'll have to remember to ask Shrubb about it later, thinks it's possibly a distant relation. Rough way to go, if a little embarrassing.

Crossing the road to the verandah, Lachlan finds he's already run out of puff, sapped by the building heat, and they find Pippa awake and sipping a cup of coffee. Addressing Shrubb, she says, 'You're up early.'

'Pigs aren't out and about, that's why.'

Her vague smile. Then she looks to Lachlan. Now in open

daylight, no longer polished by the glow of the moon, he can see the toll this hard sun has taken on her English skin. The tops of her shoulders are red and the skin is coming away in flakes like bark peeling off a minni ritchi tree. 'How'd you go?'

'Someone's busted the payphone,' Shrubb answers. Lachlan looks at him, surprised. 'Outta towners, probly.'

'Cuppa then?'

They both nod.

'How many sugars this time, Jim?'

'Make it so the spoon stands up.'

She laughs and goes into the pub. Lachlan and Shrubb survey the main street. Still no movement, and now he's standing on the edge of the green concrete, Lachlan can see most of town's layout. The community resource centre and butchery and Shire Works and deli, and a brief tier of houses beyond, abutted by a police station with a stonework tower trying to pierce the belly of sky. Ribbons of ghost gums form wriggly lines which divide all these landmarks, the sun already roasting it all at half six in the morning.

He wipes the sweat from his face on the front of his shirt. 'I've never known it to be so hot.'

'She'll hit forty-six today, you watch,' Shrubb announces, refulgent with pride. 'They're always goin' on about how Marble Bar's the hottest town on the planet. But we regularly out-scorch those bastards.'

'This isn't really a town, though. Is it?'

There you go again, Lachlan realises. *Insulting the locals.*

'Forty people live here, mate. Mainly Indigenous. And there's a handful of us whities.' He raises his pencil-thin eyebrows. 'That not a town?'

Pippa saves him by returning with two mugs of coffee. Shrubb takes his and sits on the concrete shelf, while Lachlan stands. 'You're welcome to use the phone. It's just on the wall behind the bar.'

'Thanks.' He sips. Tastes a little like dishwater and he almost says this aloud before recalling he's put his foot in it a few times already. 'In all honesty, I wanted to avoid relying on any more of your charity.'

She shrugs, returns to her own mug. 'Can't be helped.'

'I'll pay for my room. As long as I'm here. The least I can do.'

A second shrug. 'We're expensive. No other experience like it, the only pub still open in the Cliff. You sure you can afford it?'

She's so dry she doesn't even crack a smile, but he does. 'I'm sure.'

His eyes drift then, finding the back of Shrubb's head. How he perches there like a stone monument, peering out on his town with love. Out onto the strange plaques just across the road, sending another shiver through Lachlan; that conglomerate shadow he saw rearing up in the corner of his eye.

The Rift.

He finds Pippa's eyes. 'Shrubb says Toby was looking for something out here.' Dry as she is, he sees the moment all humour drains from her expression. 'The Rift, or whatever?' Takes a sharp breath. 'So, what is the Rift?'

She explains it the best she can, the best Toby had articulated it to her. Lachlan hangs there transfixed as the heat intensifies. She can always hear the furnace building as clearly as she feels it brushing against her skin. How the corrugated iron starts to shift like nerves jumping under flesh. How the grass rasps as the legless lizards ramble through.

All the while Shrubb doesn't turn back to them once, not even after he's finished his coffee, but just watches whatever might happen today in Jasper Cliff.

Pippa explains that, yes, Toby had gone to Cue in the hope he might feel the spark of inspiration for his first novel. And he wasn't there very long before he found something very different. Driving out near the Dalgaranga Meteorite Crater, he found an ancient clump of breakaway country, used by Chinese prospectors to grow their vegetables to sell at market back in the day. Toby explained that he found this weird granite boulder with a hole in it. When he got real close to that boulder, he saw something.

'Saw what?' Lachlan asks.

Toby had described it as a vision of sorts. It was more like time travel, crazy as it sounds. He said it was like being pitched back a century ago. He saw something which had happened near those granite boulders.

'He thought it had something to do with his epilepsy,' Pippa says.

Lachlan shakes his head. 'Our Nan. When we were little, she got into our heads. Tried to convince us our seizures were something else. Like we were bloody prophets or some crazy shit.' He turns to include Shrubb in this. 'One too many doobies back in the day.'

Shrubb frowns. 'A prophet?'

'Someone who can see into the past, the future. Fairytale crap.'

Toby had told Pip he couldn't sleep the night after so, as soon as daylight broke, he jumped back in the car and went out east of

Cue to find the same outcrop again. But he couldn't. Almost like it had vanished overnight. Something which could manifest itself and disappear again out in the mulga at will.

Shrubb returns to watching. He watches the truncated carriage of the school bus do its rounds, pulling up outside houses behind the deli. Sometimes kids file on, sometimes they don't.

'Did he tell you?' Lachlan asks. 'Exactly what he thought he saw?'

Toby had said he saw a young Chinese woman give birth. It was bizarre, but perhaps his brain had misfired during the seizure, made him think he saw something when it was just background nerve-endings blazing like mad, brewing up a stew of nonsense, wild and ridiculous as a fever dream. So he went back into Cue and started searching. By the end of the day, he found her name.

'What he saw had really happened,' Pippa explains, watching Lachlan's glassy eyes widen. 'There was a record of it. Her family had brought her and the child into Cue to be checked over by someone they trusted, a nurse in the mining camp. December, eighteen ninety-eight.'

'That's impossible,' Lachlan blurts.

Toby spent the next few weeks searching for more information on this girl and her baby. It was a hard trot considering most of the Chinese prospectors kept to themselves. What he did eventually uncover disturbed him. Because the family had established their garden in that area of breakaway country, there was more than one account of prospectors experiencing the exact same thing Toby had.

'They started to think it was haunted,' Pippa says. 'So they abandoned the garden just a couple of months later. Packed up all their stuff and bolted.'

The uncle of the young woman Toby had seen give birth had been subject to most of these *hauntings*. This made sense when it turned out he spent more time at the garden granites than any of the others. He'd claimed he'd had a vision about one of the local constables hurting a young girl in her hut one night.

Pippa set her jaw tight. 'That girl turned out to be his niece.'

The girl's uncle showed up ranting and raving in Cue and quickly disappeared into the gaol. Toby managed to dig up the record of his transfer to an asylum in Perth. After all, a Chinese man accusing a white police constable of rape wasn't ever going to go much further than the inside of his cell. He was dead by the end of the month. Cause of death not stated.

Lachlan runs both hands down his pallid face. 'Right. Okay. This is a lot to take in.' He looks at Shrubb but still Shrubb keeps watch over town. 'What's any of this got to do with Toby showing up here?'

Pippa tells him when word spread about the garden granites being a place where people saw things – whether they liked it or not – locals of Cue started going out there to check it out. Miners from town would take their sweethearts out there to spook them into a kiss or two. One of these was an Italian mason who'd just landed in Cue from further north.

'All the way from Jasper Cliff,' Shrubb adds.

Pippa sidles up beside Lachlan, and she's disturbed by how little he looks like Toby this morning. Surely yesterday she had yearned to see his face as similar to Toby's, seen what she'd wanted to see. She points over town to the burnished stonework of the police station's tower.

'He was part of a stonemason's group who shipped out

here from Rome to work on the construction of government buildings,' she tells Lachlan. 'The Cliff was their first job. Cue was their second. Over seven hundred kilometres apart.'

So when the mason arrived in Cue and heard all these stories about so-called hauntings in the garden granites, he knew exactly what they were talking about. He'd heard much the same thing while working in Jasper Cliff. He'd seen the same thing in Jasper Cliff.

'Prospectors called it *the Rift*,' Pippa tells him. 'The goldrush kicked off around 1890, and there were rumours about it right from the start. Toby really got stuck into the research. I used to say he could write his novel based on everything he'd collected, or even some non-fiction, but I don't think that really mattered to him anymore. He was under its spell. Looked like a man smitten, you know?' Then rethinks this. 'Infatuated, even.'

The rumours started as there was a patch of foothills in the Barite Range the local Nyamal people wouldn't go anywhere near. They warned the prospectors and fossickers to stay away too. Said the Afghan cameleers had set loose some kind of oracle years earlier. It was supposed to lead them through the deserts but had become dangerous. The blackfellas called it the intruder.

'*Intruder*?' Lachlan asks.

'Toby wasn't sure about the translation to English,' Pippa says. 'But it's the closest he could find to the Nyamal word.'

By the time the stonemasons arrived in 1895, the Rift had really worked up a reputation as being haunted, and this same worker who ended up in Cue went searching for it. Guess he had a taste for the macabre.

'Can't blame him,' Pippa adds. 'Growing up Catholic. Our

religion can get pretty morose sometimes. Sets a bit of a tone for the rest of your life.'

'And did he find it?' Lachlan asks. 'The Rift?'

Pippa nods.

She peers down at Shrubb watching a willie wagtail and a crow pecking at each other in the main street's centre nature strip. A Nyamal woman in an East Pilbara Shire uniform walks past a house by the ramshackle butchers and a pit bull launches itself at the fence, snarling at her. The old white man watering his lawn sees this, sees who his dog is growling at. Then smirks.

Shrubb snaps, 'Dave Sedden is such an old cunt.'

Watching the Nyamal woman hurry on to get away from the snarling pit bull, Pippa sees the Bernese mountain dog in that yard instead, how its leviathan head emerged like a sea god's from the bloodied ocean, its brow thatched with cow gore.

Shrubb looks back at them. 'He's trained that dog to have a go at blackfellas. I can walk past that fence no hassles and the mongrel won't make a peep.'

'Did Toby find it too?' Lachlan cuts in.

Pippa shakes her head. 'He tried.'

'Tried for most'a the time he was here,' Shrubb says, turning to the main street again, falling back out of the conversation.

'For about five months straight,' Pippa resumes. 'See, we managed to get a hold of the stonemason's account of what he saw. He wrote about it in a letter to one of his countless sweethearts here in town. He even wrote down what the Rift looks like but didn't say exactly where he found it. Only that it's somewhere in the foothills along the Coongan River.'

Pippa points to the rolling shapes of the Barite Range, encircling the town and already quivering with morning heat. 'For five months straight, Toby set out into those hills every single day. Sometimes in forty-five degrees. At first, I thought he was just committed.' Clears her throat to admit this next bit, 'Took me a while to realise it was more like obsession.'

Lachlan turns to her. 'Then why'd he stop?'

She frowns. 'Sorry?'

'You said he was out there every day all that time. So what stopped him after five months? Why'd he stop looking for the Rift?'

The answer must be naked on her face, and Lachlan says, 'Because of you. He stopped because of you.'

Pippa nods then, can't help the smile pinch in the corner of her mouth. 'Yeah, I'd never thought about it like that,' she admits. 'But I think you're right.'

I guess I saved him from himself. It's a pleasant thought, but then Pippa looks at Lachlan again: Lachlan and not-Toby. *For a while anyway.*

He leans against the bar most of the morning, begging with strangers in the nearest regional centre for help and understanding, with little success. When he asks Pippa why the aircon isn't switched on, she simply smiles, 'Hasn't worked for yonks. Been waiting for someone to come out from the coast to fix the bloody thing.' The smile on her face sours. 'Not everyone's that keen to come out and visit the Cliff. As I'm sure you're beginning to understand.'

By ten in the morning, Lachlan's ready to strip his shirt off.

And he can hear how the building heat is making his voice thinner, irascible over the phone, as yet another business informs him Jasper Cliff is just too far away to send a tow truck; it simply wouldn't be worth the trip financially.

About an hour later, Lachlan has to continuously adjust his hold on the receiver as it keeps slipping from his sweaty fingers, and then Glen walks in with Pippa. Lachlan's in the middle of arguing with a mobile mechanic when he sees the grave looks on their faces. He hangs up the phone without thinking.

Glen grimaces, his limp a little less severe than yesterday. Though he does pause to scratch irritably at his calf muscle. 'I went for a drive this mornin',' he explains. 'Just to check up on ya car, Lachie. Only just got back actually.'

Somehow, he already knows what Glen's about to say. Can see it in how Pippa refuses to meet his eyes.

'The FIFO pricks round here, they get bored,' Glen goes on, as if this is some explanation. 'Guess there's only so many pornos ya can watch on loop before ya go lookin' for thrills elsewhere.'

'How bad is it?'

Glen shakes his head. 'It's totalled, Lachie. Windows were taken to with a cricket bat by the looks of it. All the wheels are gone. Even ya spare.'

'I can't believe this is happening,' Lachlan tells the bar, breathing too hard. 'I still owe repayments on that car. Shenille too. We got it together.' Glances up at them. 'My fiancée.'

'I'm sorry, champ,' Glen tells him. 'There wasn't much we could do. That road's notorious for this kinda thing. It could've been picked apart within an hour of us leavin' it behind.'

'We'll figure something out,' Pippa says, trying to soothe his climbing panic. 'Don't stress. Like I said, you're welcome to stay here as long as you need.'

Lachlan glares at the pub phone a while, considers breaking the receiver across the bar, but what's the point? Won't make him feel any better; didn't last time with the payphone. And it won't put his car back together.

When he looks up again, he sees Glen and Pippa are still watching him. He strides for the scalding sunshine outside. 'Think I need a drink.'

When Glen pulled up in the Triton along Munjina–Roy Hill Road earlier that morning, he couldn't help but chuckle to himself to find Lachlan's Falcon completely untouched.

This road had a reputation. Leave your car overnight and by morning it'd be a shell, picked over for parts. *Lucky little bastard*, Glen thinks with a smile.

After stepping from the car, he stooped below the hairy mulga to look over the Falcon. Even ran his fingers along its side. A flash of cupping Lachlan's head in his hands yesterday above the red mud road. The young man's jerking body – each time his head tried to writhe free and hammer against the sharp rocks. Glen's pitted hands the only obstacle to further harm. The feeling of safety, of care. Not something he was used to. Felt nice to help someone, to make some good in this world.

He let his hand drop from the side of the Falcon, then his eyes strayed down the road. Nothing from Auski Roadhouse way, nothing from Nullagine the other side. Just him and the car where he found Lachlan. He liked seeing the kid in Pippa's pub.

The way he and young Pippa were already making puppy-dog eyes at each other, even if they weren't entirely conscious of it themselves. How June took an easy shine to him too. He'd make a nice little addition to their pub family, especially now it looked like Toby had shot through for good.

Glen tried to recall the last true friend he had, before Pippa, June and Shrubb. It was so long ago he's surprised it hadn't fogged out of all recognition. Hannah Parslow. Literally the girl next door. When her family first moved in, Glen couldn't understand a word any of the buggers were saying. Their Pommy accents were that thick. Yorkshire, he thinks they were from Yorkshire.

But then he'd wander into the backyard and find Hannah straddling the HardiePlank fence, locks bobbing golden with the hard city light. A bold blue sky as if she might plummet into it instead of toppling the other way and smack into the wild oats on Glen's side of the yard. It'd only been a couple days of them riding their bikes up and down the driveway before Mum started in on him.

'You two are so lovely together,' she crooned, pinching Glen's blushing cheek. 'I'll be a grandmother before I know it.'

But in truth, Glen had never seen Hannah in that way. Even in the years which followed, even as he saw how the other boys chased Hannah around with their eyes. Glen got his thrill from other things. And most of those things were buried out behind the shed.

The shed, that's what brought it all tumbling down. He should've never let Hannah into the shed. But she'd begged him. She'd catch him stepping from the rattly tin door nearly every afternoon, and he'd beam at her straddling the HardiePlank with that loveable smile on her lips. 'What you do in there all day, Glen?'

The day he relented, the day he let her in on his little secret, was the day it all came crashing down. He'd let out a big sigh for show but then led her inside, let her be encompassed by the reek of loose hay and mouse shit. And then he took his tools from the cupboard with the wonky door. All the tools he'd been coupling together from scraps for years. A piece of wood snaggled with rusted nails. A freshly sharpened axe-head affixed to a sturdy length of timber. Old knives buffed back into gleaming.

He showed Hannah the rubber grips he'd added. 'So they don't slip outta ya hand, see?'

Her face said it all. 'So they don't slip out of your hand when you're doing what exactly?'

Once she'd hurried back out of the shed, Glen noticed she didn't even hang around to watch him clip the padlock back on. He asked if he'd see her tomorrow and she mumbled a maybe and vaulted over that HardiePlank fence agile as one of the local neighbourhood cats Glen had been disappearing for years.

Glen stared at the Falcon again, the wet windows showing back only the glum sky and not his reflection. It wasn't so much that Hannah had been scared of him, ignored him and avoided him after he showed her the weapons he'd been making, it was the betrayal of trust. He'd decided to share this most intimate thing with her, and she hadn't even tried to hide her disgust from him.

He wasn't planning on fucking up the Falcon. But then he looked down and saw a decent-sized branch had broken off the mulga tree beside him, either last night or the one before. Still sturdy as all hell. He considered the prospect of Lachlan leaving town so soon and leant down to take the fallen tree limb, felt his sore knee ping, felt the throb of the python's fang marks in his calf muscle.

Couldn't say he had a particularly good time taking the Falcon apart, letting the air out of each tyre – even the spare – and then unplugging random valves in the engine. All means to an end. He couldn't let Lachlan leave again so soon. He liked the kid. Liked that feeling of having done some good in this world. So there wasn't any harm in keeping him around just a little longer. No harm in that at all.

It's never too late to start making new friends.

Then he swung the branch of mulga through the back pane, watching it shatter in a spray of tiny, blue breadcrumbs.

5

They watch Lachlan return half an hour later from the deli, a longneck bottle of Woodstock in hand. Pippa's throat tightens to see this. She suspects it might actually be his second with how he stumbles on the footpath, bangs a shoulder against the Colorbond fence.

'Idiot,' Glen observes. 'Should we call the cops on him? Drink-walkin's still illegal if I'm not mistaken.'

Pippa glances down at Shrubb, who's now sitting in his own camp chair on the verandah, after retreating from the blistering sunlight edging hour by hour closer to their feet. 'You'd hope people would be more resilient,' she adds angrily. 'How has he given up already?'

She watches Lachlan zombie past the ghost gum without glancing at Aunty Belle; she doesn't see him pass by, staring down at the lawn and muttering to herself like she's whispering canticles to the broiling wind.

Once he's within five metres of the pub verandah, Pippa steps out into the feverish light. 'Nup. You can wrack off with that.'

Lachlan freezes on the spot, scowling at her. 'With what?'

Crosses her arms, looks at the bottle.

'Eh?' Dumbfounded. 'It's a pub.'

'No BYO,' Glen adds, then chuckles.

Lachlan drinks. 'Silly rule.'

Pippa glances back at Shrubb; he shows no hint of conceding anything. But she can never be sure with Shrubb. He hides so much of the pain behind those bloodshot eyes.

'I would've just bought it from here if I thought you'd let me,' Lachlan snaps at her. Now he's standing motionless in the yellow blaze, they can all see him shrinking before their eyes. 'I thought you were helping me out?'

'Not if you plan to drink your troubles away.' She points back down the road where the sprinklers are busy missing the lawn and watering the footpath instead. 'Finish it before you come back here.'

'S'bullshit,' Lachlan says, sighing heavily. 'No difference anyway between there and out here with the aircon fucked.'

'You'd be surprised,' she tells him. 'And you're about to find out.'

'Absolute bullshit.'

He does a full three-sixty, potters away. Lifts the Woodstock bottle and slurps.

Pippa senses Glen edge up beside her. 'That might've been a bit hard on the poor bloke.'

'Too bad. I don't want him drinking around Jim.'

'I'm fine,' Shrubb says without looking at them. 'I don't need ya to babysit me, Pip. S'fine.'

'Ya right, aren't ya Shrubby?' Glen asks, scratching at his calf again, struggling to balance on one leg while he does it.

'I don't crave it no more.'

'See, he doesn't crave it no more.'

'I don't care.' She stews, chewing nothing, jaw working around. Then looks at Glen hopping. 'You got ants in your pants or something?'

'Think I got bitten by a spider last night.'

Pippa turns to watch Lachlan trundle back down the scorching footpath again. Watches him stop in the spray of the sprinkler a moment, letting his bare legs get coated. Watches him drink some more from the bottle. 'He should know better than to feel sorry for himself,' she says.

There's a quiet Nyamal woman in a tangerine dress sitting under a ghost gum in the middle of the main street and Lachlan finds himself standing beside her. With his shadow cast across her silver head of hair, she looks up at him, expressionless. Unsurprised. Sees now she's not as old as he first thought, in her forties maybe, probably only a few years older than June. So he wonders why she's gone grey so early.

'It's bloody hot,' Lachlan says, as if the woman doesn't know. As if he can't see where she's sweated through her dress.

He slumps beside her. 'My little brother's gone,' he tells her. 'Toby. Tobias. Could always tell he was going to be an author, eh? With a name like that. Sort of arty-farty, isn't it? *Tobias*.'

Lachlan looks up at the woman again and she holds his eyes. 'Did you know him?' he asks her. 'Toby?'

The woman gives no sign that she's understood him, or even heard him.

'What's your name?' he asks this time.

After examining him closely, the woman finally makes a move.

She reaches over so carefully it's like he's watching her in slow motion. She easily uproots the Woodstock bottle from his grasp and places it aside. Then hands him the water bottle from next to her.

'I have no idea where he is. Where he's gone,' Lachlan says, now grasping the water bottle. 'Is this a place where people go missing?'

The woman touches her lips, then shakes her head.

'What's that?'

Now she lifts both hands and her slightly bent fingers form into a phalanx of shapes and symbols.

He cottons on too slow. *She's deaf.*

'Bugger, I'm sorry.'

The woman smiles, then taps the water bottle in his hand with her index finger. Makes another hand sign.

'Yeah, I'm a dipshit, aren't I?' he asks.

The woman smiles harder, nods.

Lachlan searches for shade in the stiff grass of a gully behind the deli, but most of the ghost gums here are undersized. He lazes in their shadows but even the loam has warmed up, and when he lies down it's like stretching out on an electric blanket. Now he's alone, he takes the hip flask from his pocket, the one he purchased from the deli at the same time as the bottles of Woodstock, and sips.

Above the high bank, he can see the stonework tower the Italian stonemasons fixed together when the town was new and burgeoning. Lachlan waddles up towards it, swaying like he could tumble at any minute. Bangs his fists on the front door of the police station, as he can hear an aircon running inside. But then his eyes find the notice through the glass: *This station is not manned 24 hours. Dial 000 for emergencies.*

'This is a bloody emergency,' Lachlan says.

He only left the Nyamal woman under the ghost gum twenty minutes ago, and already he doesn't think he can take another twenty minutes of this. Didn't know his body could produce so much sweat. That cruel pinball of sunlight appears to hang directly above him, as if saving the worst of its punishment for Lachlan, and Lachlan alone. This bleeding sweat to death, his penance.

When he finally reaches the pub again, Pippa and Glen and Shrubb haven't moved an inch. Been watching him wandering around like a fuckwit presumably. By now the unrelenting blaze has extinguished most good sense in his head and he can feel himself close to fainting.

'Feelin' a bit average, are we?' Glen asks.

'I'm not drinking anymore,' he tells Pippa, opening both hands to prove it. 'Can I please come in now?'

Tries his hardest not to be peeved at her crabby expression. 'You'll probably still reek of it though.'

Shrubb looks at her over his shoulder. 'I don't need ya to protect me, Pip,' he tells her softly. 'Told ya I'm okay, and I meant it.'

Before Pippa can give him the go-ahead, Glen's stepped out of the cool shade of the verandah and taken Lachlan by the arm. 'Beatin' yaself up isn't goin' to help nothin'. Ya know that, don't ya?'

Lachlan lets himself get towed along with Glen and when they hit the shadow of the pub's overhang, he trembles with relief.

Shrubb must note the expression on his face. 'Coolest spot in the Cliff, mate. Everyone knows it.'

'Everyone without a working aircon, that is,' she adds, addressing Shrubb and Glen, but can't remove her judgemental eyes from Lachlan.

'I need a shower,' Lachlan says as he slumps into the closest camp chair, lounging in Glen's wet patch, and then feels the back go even slipperier with his sweat in an instant.

'No can do,' Pippa tells him, crossing her arms, with some relish.

'*Why not*?' he's about to snap but then realises it'll make him sound like even more of an entitled little shit, so he holds back.

'She's an old girl,' Pippa says, resting a hand against the cool brickwork of the pub. It's only now Lachlan notices there are large chunks of red jasper mortared into the wall alongside the grey bricks. 'The water pipes are all still galvanised steel. Never did get round to replacing them.'

Lachlan shrugs. 'So? What does that mean?'

Glen smiles. 'It means, if ya turn the shower on in this heat, the water will be so hot it'll strip the skin straight off ya back.'

'Oh, for Christ's sake.' He might make a show of his distress, but all he can do is droop uselessly in this wet chair. 'This place is fucked.'

Glen laughs. 'She'll grow on ya, champ. Trust me. She always does.'

'None of us have showers until after ten at night,' Pippa tells him. 'It's the only way you can be sure the water's cooled down enough not to give you third-degree burns.'

Lachlan looks between the three of them but can only see the back of Shrubb's head. Somehow pensive, darkly thoughtful. 'Why do you people live like this?'

Glen laughs even harder. 'Ya jokin' me, right?' Then he answers a question with a question, 'Why would ya have it any other way?'

It's too hot to fall asleep so Lachlan just sits there, his socks wet like he's stepped in a puddle. Not a single soul comes or goes along the main street. Pippa and Glen chat, sometimes go into the pub. But always return, with coffee or water, lemonade or a Corn Jack. Shrubb only moves to keep one step in front of the full scorching wave of sunlight.

Mostly Lachlan watches the deaf woman under the ghost gum who doesn't appear to move an inch. Always peering down the far side of the road, stiff in perpetual waiting.

'What's her story?' Lachlan asks. His words like desiccated husks tumbling out of his mouth, tumbleweed unfurling.

Looking at Shrubb's black curls from under his cap, wonders if he'll get an answer. 'Belle. Aunty Belle,' he says quietly. 'She's waitin' for somethin'.'

'For what exactly? A lift out of here?'

Now Shrubb looks back at him, all good humour vanquished. 'Ya should know what it's like,' he says. 'Waitin', I mean.'

At first that sounds a bit cryptic, but then wonders if he's referring to Toby.

'Or I mean, ya will soon.' Shrubb looks at the cool, green concrete under him now. 'Days like this.' He sighs. 'I get it, I really do. I honestly don't blame ya. Not one damn bit. Days like this, the only thing that'll make it better is a bloody drink.'

Lachlan rotates in his chair to find Pippa and Glen have gone back into the pub without him realising. He's glad Pippa isn't out here.

'Just one bloody drink,' Shrubb says.

Lachlan's unstuck his dry lips to say something, anything, when Pippa and Glen come back out. Pippa no longer looks splenetic, and hands him a cold bottle of water as if to confirm it. He drinks but can't remove his eyes from Shrubb now.

Until Shrubb stands, looks at Glen where he reclines in a different camp chair. Pippa must keep a few of them for when the verandah crew show up to list around and shoot the shit. 'Got any cash on ya, Glen? I left me wallet at home.'

'How convenient for you.'

'Nuh, carn. Don't be a tightarse. I know ya got some cash on ya there.'

'Shrubby, I just drove down to the big smoke and back again. The ex wanted me to go halves furnishin' me daughter's new joint in Yokine. That's slammed the savin's good and proper. How much dosh ya reckon I got till pension day?'

Shrubb's eyes turn to Pippa. Lachlan wonders how long they've known each other, some non-verbal dialogue going on between them. 'What are you going to use it for?' Pippa asks.

'What does that matter?' Shrubb bellows all of a sudden, his entire body rocking with the violent change. 'Who are you to tell me what I can and can't spend my fucken money on? You're not me daughter, Pip.'

'But it's not your money. If I'm loaning it to you, it's mine.'

He gurgles at them, thrashes off in a huff. The snap of his

thongs against cracked heels plays a strange tattoo down towards Aunty Belle under her tree.

'Goes like the clappers when he wants to, eh?' Glen remarks quietly.

'And don't go asking June for money neither!' Pippa calls out after him.

Glen looks at Lachlan. 'Done it now, Lachie.'

'What did I do?' he half-shrieks.

'Not ya fault, I spose,' he goes on. 'We shoulda warned ya is all. Shrubby's been strugglin' with the bottle fifteen years now.'

With a flummoxed expression, he waves his hands around. 'But he hangs out all day at a pub!'

Pippa looks at him with excoriating eyes. 'See a bottle of grog in there?' Now he thinks about it, he did note how the shelves above the bar were empty. Cloaked in a bluish grey coating of dust. Cool drinks on tap. Swallows awkwardly.

'When's the last time someone bought a drink from this joint, Glen?' Pippa asks.

'Must be over a year now, mustn't it?' he asks, furrowing his brow, a genuine struggle with his memory. 'I'd say about a year, yeah.'

Lachlan shakes his head, indignant. 'How was I supposed to know?' Silent a spell, thinking, blushing. 'I thought this was a pub. Not a bloody community centre where people without air-conditioning just … bloody … hang out all day!'

'Well.' Pippa re-crosses her arms, 'That's why you've got a lot to learn about Jasper Cliff.'

Shrubb returns in the seared light of evening. Usually, Lachlan might've expected the heat to concede this late in the day but it seems to intensify. Both Lachlan and Glen now sit in their camp chairs shirtless, allowing the material to soak up their perspiration; Glen's tan-sleeves so dark it looks like he's dipped his arms up to the elbows in molasses.

The galahs chirp weirdly along the footpath, garish like Mardi Gras birds, and part for Shrubb as he comes stumbling back. 'Yep,' Glen comments. 'He's on the piss again.'

Shrubb tries to lean against the verandah support and bangs his head against it a little. Then attempts to recover as if Lachlan and Glen might not've seen. 'Boys. What's goin' on?'

'Sit down,' Glen says, his voice as soft and hurt as Lachlan's ever heard it. 'It's too hot to get a load on, mate.'

'Haven't. I'm fine. Like I keep tellin' you fuckers.'

Glen glances back into the pub. 'Pippa's cleanin' up the pie heater now mate, but if she comes out and sees ya like this, ya know she's goin' to give June a bell.'

'She reckons she's me fucken daughter or somethin'.' That last word comes out slick with spit. 'But she's not. Me fucken daughter. When she gunna get that through her thick skull, Glen?'

Lachlan has rarely seen another human being this drunk; the feeling of someone swinging a meat cleaver around recklessly inside his chest. He did this, whether he meant to or not.

'Sit down, mate,' Lachlan offers half-heartedly.

'Don't call me fucken *mate*. I've known you like five seconds. I'm not ya mate.'

Shrubb's weedy, but once the anger gets him, he goes rigid and ropey, like he could lash out fast as a snake. Lachlan flinches.

'Oi, cool ya jets,' Glen says, his voice still soft, almost soothing. 'He's just bein' friendly. He's worried about ya. Same as I am.'

'It's Pip. She's always talkin' to me like I'm a hopeless case, ya know?'

'She's just worried about ya too. More worried than the rest of us.'

'Talkin' to me like she's me daughter. She's not.'

'She just cares about ya.'

'Not me daughter.'

They fall into an awkward silence then, and Glen scrapes the thirsty flies from his sweat-matted beer belly. Jasper Cliff glows hot red, a miscellany of corrugated iron and other people's lives, and at this hour it's almost like they can see every tiny detail of it. It's a toy-town, and they're pale giants. A house a couple of roads back from the heritage police station starts to thump with loud music, a subwoofer booming its guts out into the near dark.

'Bit of a shindig at the Neave place tonight,' Shrubb explains, eyes struggling to focus on anything at all. 'Think I'll swing by.'

'Carn, don't ya think ya've had enough for today?' Glen implores. 'Don't ya think ya punished yaself enough?'

'Just a coupla drinks.'

'Pip'll let ya take a room. Why don't ya sleep it off, eh?'

From up here, they can see the winding roads, where the ghost gums punctuate the edges of searing bitumen. Figures coming to and from the Neave house. The windows now lit.

Shrubb nods to himself. 'Just go for a coupla drinks, and then I'll be back, boys.'

Glen watches him start to walk away, his voice choked when he calls out, 'Don't go, Shrubby.'

But Shrubb's thongs are already flapping across the street. Belle looks on from under her waiting tree.

Watching those sweaty black curls against the back of Shrubb's neck, Lachlan can't help but want to wriggle out of his sweaty, cooking skin. 'Shit, Glen,' he mutters quietly, now inspecting the green concrete between his feet. 'I didn't know. I wouldn't have had a drink in front of him if I'd known.'

'Not your fault, old son,' he says, watching Shrubb go with sad eyes. 'It's his battle. His alone. Only he can drag himself out the other side.'

When Pippa steps back out, she's sweated through her singlet so Lachlan can see the dark straps of her bra. 'Was that Jim?'

'Just missed him,' Glen informs her. 'There's a party at the Neave house. Said he was goin' to swing by over there.'

'How was he?'

Glen flinches. 'Skunked.'

'That's it, I'm callin' June.'

'Keeps on about how ya not his daughter, love. Maybe ya should go a bit easier on him?' He shifts in his chair, and Lachlan can see the sweat-shadow of his shape stamped on the material. 'Think that's what gets him so torn up sometimes. I think he *is* startin' to think of ya as a daughter. Means he might have to eventually let go of the other one. Let go of any hope he has left.'

'I'm not worried about any of that,' Pippa tells him, makes back inside for the phone behind the bar. 'I just don't want him to take a fall on the way home and crack open his skull on the bloody road.'

Sunset makes a fiery show behind the Barite Range, while Jasper Cliff is lost to the darkness in the shadow of the low hills. Most of the houses along the road behind the police station are lit with tawny light but only the Neave joint thumps and rattles, strangers cheer and shout. Lachlan stops drinking from his ice-cold water bottle, the fourth of today Pippa's brought out to him, and decides to pour it over his head instead.

Glen sees this. 'Now that's the way.'

The next time Lachlan stares down the main road, he sees the lawn under the ghost gum is empty; the deaf woman he was babbling to drunkenly earlier must've slipped away. Instead, he watches June marching down the footpath. She kicks a hose attached to a sprinkler roped across her way.

'Where is he?' she snaps at Glen when she arrives at the pub.

He simply nods. Even from all the way back here, they can hear the music getting louder, some country and western twang. Lachlan can feel the throb of it with his bare feet glued to the warm concrete.

'Silly bastard,' she gargles, then frowns at Lachlan fleetingly, to see him dripping wet after tipping the water bottle over himself. 'And he's been doin' so well this year.'

'Not the first time he's fallen off the wagon. Won't be the last either.'

Now Pippa's hanging onto the pub doorway again, Lachlan feels his throat tighten. Doesn't want her to tell June it was him and the bottle of Woodstock which got Shrubb going again. His cheeks rosy up with shame, despite the cold water beaded all over his face.

'Yeah, but I can make sure he gets back up on that fucken wagon quick smart.'

She takes out her mobile phone as Glen saunters past her. Lachlan watches him go, a little surprised to see something seemingly immobile jolt back into movement. As June taps at her mobile, Glen wanders over to the sprinkler and hose June kicked on her way over. He turns off the tap it's attached to. Then disconnects the hose from the tap, and from the sprinkler the other side. He lets the surplus water spill out, then loops the green hose around one shoulder.

'Hell are ya doin'?' Pippa sings out.

With a satisfied grin, he poses in front of them. 'Let's do this.'

June looks more than a little miffed. 'There's an easier way.'

He sighs, lets the hose slacken to the warm concrete. 'Jokin'? And here I was thinkin' I would get to blast him again.'

'Carrot and stick, mate.' Shakes her head at him in disgust. 'Let's at least try the carrot first.'

She holds the mobile to her ear. Someone picks up on the other end. 'That you, Daisy? Yeah, it's June. Yeah. Nup, at the pub, love.' Now all three of them watch June, tightening with expectation. 'Shrubb's there with ya, isn't he? Carn, don't lie to me now, Daise. He's there, isn't he?'

She listens. Looks at Pippa. Raises her eyebrows.

'I'm gunna need ya to send him back over to us.' Stops and listens again. 'Coz he's an alcoholic, that's why.' Listens more. 'Not drinkin', that right? My arse, he's not. Send him along home, Daise.'

Glen turns to Lachlan, nods down at the hose. 'She let me blast him with this last time.'

'I know he's a grown man, but he also can't help himself and next time ya brother wants to ply him with grog ya get him to give me a call first.' June winks at Pippa. Finally, some relief on Pippa's expression as it cracks into a smile. 'I tell ya what. That lovely nephew'a mine's comin' all the way from the coast next week to take me shoppin'. If ya send Shrubb home now, I'll take ya with us. How's that?'

Silence, and June breathing into the phone.

'All expenses paid.'

A little bit more silence. Then June grins, hangs up. She looks at a disappointed Glen. 'See, no need for the stick this time. Plus, ya have too much fun with it.'

They watch the grass block for a while as the music keeps thudding in the ground. Watch the ghost gum–freckled gully. Lachlan wipes the water from his eyes and within ten minutes, two men in pale singlets and Shrubb come shambling out of the gloom of the spare block; Lachlan hears them before he sees them, hears Shrubb's hurried, flapping thongs. Once they reach the pub, Lachlan can see the men have basically dragged Shrubb all this way.

'Hands off me!' Shrubb bellows now, wrestling his way free.

'Aunty Daisy says she's really sorry, Aunt June,' one of the young men says.

'Tell her that's just fine.' June can't help but beam. 'Tell her I'll give her a bell about the details on the weekend.'

The two young men say goodnight and turn to make their way back across the spare block.

Glen calls out, 'How was the party?'

'Piss off you sheep-fucking prick,' Shrubb spits, his moods far more inclement after he's been on the sauce.

'Now, now, don't get touchy.'

Pippa walks up to the edge of the concrete, 'You okay, Jim?'

'Why'd ya call her for?' he whines, glancing at June.

'I was just worried about you, that's all. Wanted to make sure you got home safe. Don't want a repeat of that broken arm a couple of years back.'

His face goes rigid for a moment, as if he means to start calling her all kinds of names like he just did Glen, but then Pippa chucks him a towel. It hits him in the chest before he manages to catch it with fumbling hands, then starts mopping at his sweaty face. 'Cheers.'

Pippa nods into the pub. 'I've done up the bed in the room next to Lachlan. Go sleep it off.'

But he just hangs there a spell longer, shoulders slouched, and it looks like he's fallen asleep on his feet. Then Lachlan realises, this is shame; he can't bring himself to look at June or Pippa. In response to this, June runs her hand over the back of his neck, fingers teasing under the brim of his cap, and kisses him gently on the cheek.

'It's okay, bubby. You're safe. Everyone's safe,' she whispers, still loud enough for the three watchers to hear. 'Go rest now, eh?'

He still doesn't look at any of them, steps onto the verandah.

'Sweet dreams,' Glen says.

'You're fucked in the head.'

'That's rude.' He looks at Lachlan in shock. 'Very bloody rude.'

Pippa walks down onto the footpath to join June now. They chat quietly, so quietly Lachlan can't hear what's being said, and June stands on the rolled-up hose, still burping water up onto the road.

Lachlan turns to Glen, sweat lubricating his twisting motion in the camp chair. 'They seem close,' he says. 'June and Shrubb.'

'They oughta be,' Glen tells him. 'They were married for ten years.'

June decides to hang around, join the three of them in the blistering night, when a blaze of high beams burns across the ghost gum under which Aunty Belle waits during the day. Pippa catches it in the corner of her eye, the tree suddenly luminescent.

The music is even louder at the Neave house now and Pippa's throat clenches all on its own to watch a police paddy wagon ease back to fifty and cruise into town. The high beams die, and they watch the blue chequers with some portent cross before the pub.

'Bloody ridiculous.' Glen throws his hands up in the air. 'Whitefellas chuck a party, they can go till midnight. The Neaves do the same thing …' He looks down at the watch on his wrist, 'It's shut down at eight-thirty.'

Jasper Cliff awash in absolute night, they can track the paddy wagon navigating street after street so clearly from back here, watching those headlights like a lantern dropped into some perpetual darkness, how it falls in slow motion, only weaves here and there.

What if you've been wrong all this time? a voice not quite her own asks Pippa, sousing her in terrible dread.

Seeing that chessboard of marks on the side of the paddy wagon, she can't help but wonder. When Toby disappeared, she'd taken it personally. Just accepted it had something to do with him not wanting kids. Them screaming at each other like they had, saying the stuff neither really meant.

So he'd taken off. Scissored the bond between them so she wouldn't be tethered to him any longer. Leaving her free to find another, someone not so appalled at the mere prospect of becoming a father.

But now Lachlan's ruined everything with his doubt. She looks down at him, useless and pouring more sweat than the rest of them, a sad shadow of his little brother. She can't imagine where Toby might be.

'They woulda had to come all the way from the Bar, eh?' Glen asks, wrenching her back into the moment. 'Bit of a drive just to shut down a little party.'

'I bet that old wanker Dave Sedden called them,' June adds.

Now a laser of hot white light cuts through the Neave place. Pippa has to blink against the flare. A spotlight scything from the paddy wagon and blazing through the front windows of the party house. The thumping music quickly dies. Graveyard silence falls over the night. Pippa can hear her own scared breath.

'Well, that's that then,' June declares in a defeated kind of way.

The pillar of glary light continues to rove all over the house, as if searching for something. *The truth perhaps*, Pippa wonders. The truth about where Toby might be, alive or dead. The paddy wagon slowly cruises away, and the spotlight slashes through a patch of river red gums. It rambles through the droughty trees and Pippa watches intently with slightly watering eyes, as if the truth might be uncovered at the tip of that searching godlike finger.

Pippa steps from the verandah, seen enough now. She stands next to June, and without a word, she picks up the curled hose and starts back down the footpath towards where Glen had taken it. No one watches her do this, not June or Glen or Lachlan, fixated with the spotlight searching out the raggier edges of town.

She doesn't exactly care that Glen took the hose – the shire has a thousand of them – but it's something to do, something to shake the dread sticking, insistent as the sweat, to her English-ceramic skin. Weak skin, that of the English, she's realised since coming to this place. Nowhere near hardy enough.

She unravels the hose, reconnects one end to the cheap sprinkler on the lawn. Over here in sheerer darkness, she can track the progress of the paddy wagon back towards them much more clearly. That spotlight now stiffens up against the stars, a burning pillar, swinging around aimlessly.

Too busy bullying blackfellas to be out there looking for Toby.

She tries to wrestle against the gruesome slideshow in her mind, but here it is. A bad idea to separate herself from the verandah and the others, because out here in the shadows, her fears rumble; a stampede of frightened stock in her chest.

She wonders where he is, where he might've ended up, because she often noticed how he shrank whenever a mean-looking truckie showed up at the bowsers. Or a tattooed, gym-junkie miner raised his voice inside the pub. Toby was sensitive, too sensitive to put up much of a fight.

That made him vulnerable to exactly the types of men she was afraid of. Vulnerable to what happened to her in The Glenmore Hotel. It happened to girls and women, most of all, that much is undeniable. But it happened to men and boys too.

No, you're overthinking this, Pippa tries to tell herself. *Just stop it. This isn't going to help anyone. Least of all Toby.*

She can't tell where that enormous energy came from, when she placed her thumb against that bastard's eye in The Glenmore and told him he'd lose it if he kept taking what he wanted to take from her. She also can't guess what might've happened if she hadn't discovered such fire at that very moment; can't guess what might've happened to Toby, out there on the road by himself, if he happened to catch the eye of some dreadful roamer.

As if trying to swallow the bad thoughts, her throat tightens as she drags the hose back to the tap by the footpath, seeing the spotlight blaze into the main street as the paddy wagon cruises towards them. The beam slices through the dusty windows of each dead building, searching for the slightest sign of life.

As she kneels to attach the other end of the hose to the tap, Pippa crinkles her eyes shut and searches for him. For Toby. Finds his touch so easily, even after all these weeks he's been gone. 'It's okay,' she tells herself. 'He'll be okay.'

When Pippa opens her eyes again, she sees something fluttering in the spotlight which continues to flare through abandoned homes and businesses along the main street. It flaps at her feet, catching the febrile breeze. When she looks down, it's a missing persons poster, torn from its thumbtack on the front of the deli.

The face which looks back up to her with kind eyes so familiar, heart wrenching.

Elizabeth Shrubb.

Last seen in Jasper Cliff, August 2010.

The rest of them on the verandah all turn in unison, shocked to watch another arrival in town this late. A big semitrailer bullying its way down the road. The hissy brakes fire off as it slows on its approach but the other three turn back to watch the spotlight lasering the far side of town, like visitors from another world checking the streets for any lost soul they can abduct and conduct experiments on.

When the truck pulls up, Lachlan glimpses Pippa's supine shape further along, on the nature strip, doing God-knows-what. He's about to call out and ask her when the semitrailer's engine dies and the driver nearly cartwheels out of the driver's side door. He looks drunker than Shrubb, if that were possible. Eyes the three strangers on the pub verandah sheepishly.

The hint of a Dutch accent when he asks, 'Mind if I park here for the night?'

They all stare at him, astonished that he's made it this far. June answers for them all. 'Think ya better, mate.'

The driver shows them his thumb, staggers. 'Cheers you lot.'

But when he goes to climb back into the cab, he flounders and almost smacks onto the bitumen. Without really thinking about it, Lachlan floats from his camp chair and wanders over. Shirtless and staggering, like he's still tanked too, he watches his blackest black shadow fall against the palest of pale ghost gums.

He takes the Dutch stranger gently by his gaunt arm, feeling all the hard bones, no bicep. The truck driver turns to him with terrified eyes, as if Lachlan were about to commit the most perfidious act, betray the stranger's trust. But then Lachlan softly helps him up into the cab and feels the stranger's slim muscles lose their tightening fear.

Once the man's collapsed into the thin bed behind the truck's front seats, he looks up at Lachlan with renewed worry, his breath streaming the smell of whiskey neat. This time he grabs at Lachlan's wrist.

'Tell me,' he says, his Dutch accent even thicker now he's afraid. 'What is this place?'

Lachlan would answer the question if he had any clue. He's been asking himself the same thing since he arrived here.

'It's alright.' He pats the back of the stranger's hand. 'I don't know what this place is, but I know you're safe here.'

Watches his considerable Adam's apple do a jump as he swallows. 'But how can you be so sure of this?'

Lachlan stares into the man's frightened, drunk eyes a moment, swallows back himself. 'I don't know,' he admits. 'It's something I believe to be true.'

A prick of light in the man's eyes again, and they shimmer. Lachlan didn't know the stranger had grabbed him by the forearm again, until his grip releases and he feels all his tendons relax again.

A little tearily, the Dutchman smiles. 'I have a joke.'

Lachlan nods. 'Go on then.'

'An Australian walks into a bar and sees a Dutchman drinking. When the Australian sits down, what does he say to the Dutchman?'

'I don't know. What does the Australian say?'

'I have no fucking clue.' An awful smile spreads on the drunk Dutchman's face. 'I don't speak Australian.'

Pippa glances down the other end of the main street, after watching the semitrailer pull up. After watching Lachlan help the drunk driver back into the cab. After thinking, maybe Lachlan wasn't such a dick after all.

Hunched right outside the abandoned bakery, and as the paddy wagon cruises behind her, she watches the spotlight reach searchingly into the dark of the empty building.

Abandoned for a couple of years at least, but Pippa looks in and sees it's not empty now. The paddy wagon's spotlight blazes on the man standing inside.

Everything beyond and surrounding the bakery darkens in a heartbeat. She would scream her lungs out into the hot air if she wasn't pinned to the spot, petrified into silence.

It's Toby. She almost doesn't recognise him with how he's trembling, flaring in the paddy wagon's spotlight, his eyes so afraid like she's never seen them. He's all bloodied and garlanded with a selection of litter – crusty cat food satchels and open muesli bar wrappers stuck to his shirt.

Pippa makes a sound so full of outrage and shock it sends her hoarse. A shadow is hunched behind Toby in the spotlight, hovering in midair, the shape of an arm lodged against his back, as if there's someone just out of view, puppeting Toby.

The intruder, she thinks.

When Toby speaks, she hears a voice inside her head. And it's not Toby's voice; he's just lip-syncing. *Come find me at the Rift.* As his lips move, blood the colour of tar spills from one corner of Toby's mouth and blooms a black rose on the chest of his shirt. *I'll be waiting.*

Then the spotlight cuts away, and he's gone. Pippa collapses back onto the still-wet lawn. Whacks a hand across her mouth to stop the shrieking. Quickly jumps to her feet and looks into the bakery a second time.

Even in the dark, she can tell it's empty. Just a clutter of benches and chairs, rusting equipment left behind.

She goes to call out for June when she watches the spotlight blaze upon the three remaining outside the pub. Lachlan and Glen and June all raise their hands to shield their eyes, muttering under their breaths. Pippa searches the blazing verandah, wondering if Toby might reappear among the living.

The spotlight searches out the darkened cab of the semitrailer too but cannot locate the sleeping driver within.

Finally it dies away, leaves June standing there in the gloom showing her middle finger to the paddy wagon. 'No party goin' on here, you lot,' she calls out. 'So youse can just rack off.'

6

Days spent waiting, for what exactly Pippa's not sure.

She lacks the patience Aunty Belle appears to possess. She's watched the quiet, wordless woman under the ghost gum with wonder since she arrived in Jasper Cliff. Aunty Belle has never betrayed any trace of rage or despair or madness. Only the waiting, always the watching and waiting.

Patience is something Lachlan appears to be learning about quickly since coming here. For three days in a row, he doesn't leave the camp chair on the pub verandah. Sits there from the time he wakes around seven in the morning, until he wanders back to bed around nine at night. He only gets up to use the pub phone, to call his mum or fiancée, or to have a piss. Surrounded by Glen and Shrubb and June, he removes himself from the banter mostly, steers clear of conversation. Watches the road, raking sweat, sometimes changing his shirt around midday when it's gone water-fight wet. Pippa recognises his inertness, despises it all the same.

With his and Toby's mum having contacted the police, he says he's waiting for the cops to show up, sometimes castigating himself for not flagging them down that night they came and used the spotlight on the Neave house party. But then coming up with excuses as to why he didn't; he'd been distracted, of course, trying to do the right thing by helping the drunk truck driver back up into his cab.

This is the last place Toby was seen, these were the last people to have seen him, so surely the cops would rock up sooner or later to ask questions. Surely.

The only time Pippa sees him even mildly animated is when he gets off the phone with his fiancée. He waxes lyrical about her and shows Pippa and June photos of them together on his phone. The girl's younger than him, bleach-blonde hair and glossy, pouty lips, the tip of her tongue stuck cheekily from the corner of her mouth. Pippa knows the difference between love and lust in a man's eyes, and she's certain this is the latter.

'Don't do it, son,' Glen warns him, sipping from a glass of Pippa's lemonade. 'That furry thing between their legs will cost ya everythin' ya've got.'

Pippa winces at that. She doesn't often hear things like this come out of Glen's mouth, but when she does, she wonders if he's still holding onto some bitterness towards his ex-wife in the city.

June scowls at Glen, then nods at Lachlan. 'Don't spoonfeed him horseshit and tell him it's cornflakes.'

Glen stares at her, flummoxed. 'What's that now?'

'Who are you to be givin' out advice? Ya wife left ya for a bloody personal trainer, didn't she?'

'Me point exactly.'

'You're full'a piss and wind like the barber's cat, Glenny.'

Glen's quiet a spell. 'And he was a yoga instructor. Not a personal trainer.'

Shrubb's on the edge of the verandah, trying not to laugh.

'And you can go fuck yaself too,' Glen yells at him.

'Weren't servin' her needs, eh Glenny?' Shrubb pipes in.

June turns to him now, and asks genuinely, 'Couldn't ya find the clitoris?'

'Yeah,' Glen barks. 'I know where it's at.' He points at Lachlan. 'So does this bloke. That's why he's in a world'a trouble.'

Crows cry out like lost souls. On the third day, Pippa finds herself drifting from the others on the verandah, stepping out into the boiling point of sky, though it must only be half ten or so in the morning. Finds herself drawn to the sad croak of these crows, a murder of which jump and rock in the ghost gum above Aunty Belle down the road.

Approaching the derelict bakery, she keeps a solid few metres distance, feeling the hair spear on end along both arms. The window's dark now, no more spotlight lancing the interior to unveil Toby there, blood the colour of freshly laid bitumen spilling from his mouth. She's only distracted from her fixation with the bakery when she looks down and sees Elizabeth Shrubb staring back up at her from the footpath. Stops, checks over her shoulder to make sure the others are still preoccupied, still calling each other names, and won't notice.

Shrubb goes into the pub but then comes careening back out only moments later, overly excited. 'We've hit forty-two! We're already hotter than Marble Bar! Told ya? Didn't I tell ya?'

She reaches down and takes the flap of paper. Walks across the road without checking for cars, almost ninety-nine percent sure there won't be anything coming her way.

Aunty Belle looks up at her. She signs, *Runaway?*

Pippa tucks the flappy bit of paper under one arm. *The wind*, she signs back.

Aunty Belle nods. *Who?*

Pippa shows her the face of Elizabeth Shrubb.

Belle stares over at the pub, at Shrubb and June now laughing about this or that. She signs, *They not see?*

Pippa shakes her head. *Me put back.*

Ghost faces.

That slugs Pippa, another glimpse of what that spotlight revealed inside the abandoned bakery. The truth, perhaps? Something blacker than night, making Toby's mouth flap like a wooden puppet's: '*Come find me at the Rift.*'

Pippa signs too quickly, and Aunty Belle frowns at her. She tries again. *Toby. He searching for something.*

June said, Aunty Belle shapes each intricate motion slowly, knowing Pippa doesn't often exercise her signing. *The Rift.* She spells this last word out. *R. I. F. T.*

Do you know where it is?

Belle shakes her head. *Maybe hills by river.* She shrugs. *A ghost story.*

Pippa looks at the piece of sweat-marked paper in her hand again. Elizabeth Shrubb. Missing thirteen years now. Wait as long as they would, they might never get to the truth of this, or any of those lost faces on the deli wall. What she saw in the bakery three nights ago, even that feels unreal to her now. One more bad dream in a town beset by bad dreams.

She feels the need to move on, make for the deli again, if only to save her sanity from the horrors her imagination might summon. But quickly signs out, *Anyone else? Who found the Rift?* Spells that last word out again, same as Belle had.

Belle shrugs. *People here frightened.*

'Makes sense,' Pippa says aloud.

Then signs, *Thank you.*

Long memories here. Someone knows. Her eyes darken. *Just scared to say.*

Pippa crosses the road to the deli, gathering an obeisant pace as she reaches the flutter of missing persons posters tacked to the noticeboard. She tries not to meet any of their desperate eyes but in pinning Elizabeth's poster back to the board, she stares at the face beside it. A young, ginger bloke. Ratty little moustache and mullet; nothing out of the ordinary though. This is mining country, mullets abound.

Ricky Muswell. Missing since July 2013. She takes a spare thumbtack and sticks June and Shrubb's daughter back on the wall.

Mrs Saelim steps from the aircon gust of the deli's interior. She's muttering in Thai, likely complaining to herself about her useless husband, when she looks up with a start. 'Pip? What are you doing walking around on a day like this, Pip?'

'Hi Mrs Saelim.' Pip nods at Elizabeth Shrubb watching from on the wall.

Mrs Saelim's expression softens a little. 'I do what I can, but the wind has a mind of its own.'

'It's fine. Elizabeth is back now.'

'Oh dear.' Mrs Saelim gawks. 'Better hurry back for cover. You've already burnt that lovely British skin of yours.'

Pip looks back at her shoulders, exposed with just a singlet on. She hadn't noticed it, hadn't felt it at all, but her skin looks raw as a freshly cooked crayfish.

Lachlan likes listening to Shrubb and June and Glen, pleasant white noise. Their little debates and arguments. It distracts him from thinking about Toby, about the police still having not shown up here to begin their investigation. From here, he can see across the scattering of houses and groaning aircon units in Jasper Cliff, to the trickle of mirage on the Barite Range. Makes sense this would be a lawless place.

Today, they're arguing about what's hotter, Marble Bar or the Cliff. Marble Bar is regularly cited as being the hottest town on the planet, but Shrubb balks. After all, the mercury does not fucken lie. 'We're already hotter than the Bar and it's not even eleven o'clock yet.'

Lachlan turns to watch Pippa making her way back. Once she dumps herself into the shade, she looks down at her red-raw shoulders. 'I was out there fifteen minutes,' she says.

Lachlan nods at Aunty Belle under the ghost gum. 'She going to be okay in this heat?'

Pippa looks. 'She wouldn't say, even if she wasn't. She always brings plenty of water with her.'

'I saw you two. Doing the ...' He lifts his hands and curls his fingers into different shapes. 'Sign language thing.'

'I learned young. When we were kids back home, my uncle worked in an armaments factory in Leeds. There was an accident one day, a worker was killed. My uncle was deaf afterwards. Couldn't hear a thing if you clapped your hands an inch in front of his face. He let us do that sometimes too. All us kids learned sign so we could talk to him when he came to stay with us at Christmas. He was our favourite uncle.'

'That's good,' Lachlan says, but he's not entirely sure of what he's trying to say, looking back at Belle again in the shadow of the tree. 'That you can talk with her.'

'I'm a bit rusty. And I don't know Auslan. Sometimes I sign

something and she looks at me like I'm talking a completely different language.' Pippa laughs.

'Belle only knows Auslan coz'a her daughter,' Shrubb adds. 'They had someone who came out to the medical centre once a month just to sit with the two of them. Like two peas in a pod, those two. Only they knew what they were sayin' to each other. Get the feelin' they were bein' cheeky a lotta the time. With how they'd sign somethin' and then start gigglin' to themselves.'

Lachlan stares at Belle a moment longer, the look of calm on her expression, while he's crawling all through with what feels like hungry worms. *How can she be so fucken patient?* he thinks. *How long has she been waiting?*

'Shit. What's with the cops out here? It's been days. They even have a station here, for Christ's sake.'

'It's unmanned,' Glen says from the corner of his mouth, rubbing at a bandage on his calf. Then he continues arguing with Shrubb and June. 'The heat in the Bar is really somethin' else though, innit? Ya can't compare the two.'

'Cockie shit,' Shrubb blathers. 'It's only like seventy-five k's away. How can it be much different?'

'I'm tellin' ya. It is. Apples and bloody oranges.'

'I should've waved them down the other night,' Lachlan mumbles, mostly to himself. 'So stupid, that I didn't think to do that. That bloody drunk truckie. If I wasn't so distracted, I probably would've.'

Pippa sees him trying not to sigh. 'They'll show up,' she adds. 'Things take a bit longer out here, that's all. You're on East Pilbara Time now.'

'Meanwhile I'm just sitting here. Sweating my arse off.' *And Toby might be rotting*, he thinks.

June has detached herself from Shrubb and Glen's debate and now she meets Lachlan's eyes. 'That's the law for ya in the ol' Cliff, Lachie. The law's never been right in Jasper Cliff.'

He scowls at her. 'The hell does that mean?' He throws up his hands. 'Why is everyone in this fucken town so cryptic?'

June laughs, shares a knowing look with Pippa ever so briefly. Then she stands from her dusty camp chair, furls an index finger at him. 'Carn. Ya comin' with me,' she says, dredging up a toothy smile.

Lachlan peers at the blanched light searing the main street with dread, can't look at it without his sunnies on. 'Where?' he asks quietly.

'S'not far.'

'Should we really be walking around on a day like today?'

'What? Worried ya gunna come back lookin' like a prawn left out on the kitchen counter all day?' She rests her sweaty hand on his shoulder now, giving him just the gentlest squeeze. 'Ya safe with me. Let's go.'

As soon as Lachlan leaves the cover of the pub, he knows this is a mistake. The sky is supercharged with blue fire, and he's breathing it. They walk through the splatter of a shire sprinkler spinning and its warm droplets flecking across his bare legs can't bring an ounce of relief. He can already feel the back of his neck going raw and stretched like Pippa's shoulders.

June waves to Aunty Belle as they pass, so Lachlan gives her a shy wave too. Past the derelict second pub on the corner and across Maitland Street and through the free RV parking area with its stinky public dunnies. Now he watches a short hill, stitched with flaky lines of chert, covered in scraps left after the goldrush.

A buckled church, too, only one stone wall left standing. All this makes little sense to him, not with how June's loose dress catches a tease of wind, but none of its touch seems to bring any succour to Lachlan's frazzled brain.

'I think I should go back,' he says.

'Ya need to drink more water, son,' she tells him, squeezing his shoulder again. 'Be surprised how quick heat stroke can set in out here.'

Alongside some giant river red gums, Lachlan sees what must've once been a tributary of the Coongan River unravelling its dry tongue, but now it's no more than a sandy track choking in dead grass. June leads him up onto a flat concrete base, the stone walls long fallen away on all sides. Lachlan stubs his toe on something hard, trips, his body smacking harder into the ground.

'My toe,' he groans, deciding to just give up now, and just lie here and cook like a Christmas turkey in the sun. 'I think I've broken my toe, June.'

'Don't be silly.'

'Seriously. It's broken for sure.'

He opens his eyes again, feels the sting of sweat drip into them. Sees what he tripped on. Looks like some kind of steel ring concreted into the floor.

'See that?' June asks, following his eyes. 'That was the pin they'd attach the chains to.'

Lachlan struggles to his feet again, favouring his sore foot. He swishes around and looks. 'What?'

'When the constables showed up to keep an eye on the goldrush, they started nabbin' our old people out of these hills.' She points to the chert undulations crawling with mirage.

'Couldn't have us blackfellas runnin' around, just livin' our own lives and all that. So they would put our people in neck chains. Locked around here.' She runs a finger across her throat. 'Each one weighed twelve pounds. Made'a iron. Imagine carryin' that on ya shoulders all day.' Then she peers up at the sun. 'On a day like today.'

'I'm not sure …' Lachlan blabbers, 'if I want to hear this.'

Or know this.

'The sun might burn ya skin, sure. But imagine what havin' iron directly on it feels like.' She nods down at the pin in the concrete again. 'There'd be six to nine men in a row, all linked, and then the chains would be attached to these. And then they'd be left here all day. Shrubby says it's forty-two now, right? Pushin' forty-three. So what was it like inside here when the walls were still standin'? Three degrees hotter than that? Five?'

'They couldn't have possibly survived that.'

'See what I mean about the law in the Cliff?' June asks him, eyes softening to meet his. 'Whitefella's law. Long time ago, but it's still here. Now. Can't ya see it, Lachie? It's been and gone but it's still here. Sometimes I wish I could choose not to see it.'

He might've faceplanted into the cell floor and lost a couple of bloodied teeth against the concrete if June didn't reach out at exactly the right moment and steady him with a flat hand against his heart.

'Sometimes I wish.'

Lachlan's changed when he gets back to the pub, and not just because he's turned pale and faded – vitamin D–deficient despite the sun blazing down on Jasper Cliff. Once they reach the verandah again, Lachlan quickly rushes inside while June takes her seat near Shrubb.

'He looks a bit shaken up,' Glen comments, scratching at the slightly inflamed skin around the bandage on his leg.

'It's these young'uns today,' June explains. 'Got no idea about their own history. So when ya break it to them, it can come as a bit of a shock.'

Pippa battles the urge to go into the pub and check on him. Holds herself firm instead, planted beside the massive chunk of red rock on the concrete. Not her responsibility; he's not Toby. She knows so little about him, she's not even sure what she'd say in an attempt to comfort him.

Then he steps back out with a backpack, arming fitfully through the straps. He tries not to look at any of the four gathered there.

All the oxygen rushes from Pippa's chest. 'Lachlan, you can't.'

He meets her eyes, then glances away. 'I nabbed some water bottles out of the fridge. I hope that's okay.'

Glen waves his wide-brimmed hat at some flies. 'No one should be out in this, son. Specially someone who isn't used to it yet.' Then he looks at Shrubb and June. 'If anyone ever gets used to it.'

Lachlan ignores all this worry. 'You said Toby was looking in the hills by the river. He didn't write anything down? Tell you exactly where? He didn't keep any maps or anything like that?'

Even if he did, I wouldn't tell you, she thinks. *By not telling you, he might've saved your life.*

'Just sit down, Lachlan,' Pippa hears herself say, surprised by the tenderness in her voice, like she is talking to Toby, wherever he is. 'You have to be here for when the police arrive anyway.'

But then she sees the way he spins around and knows nothing she can say will discourage him. 'I'm done waiting,' he tells her, a shimmer of darkness rippling across the surface of his eyes.

No, he's not like Toby at all. Toby never had that look in his eyes. Toby would never look at me like that.

'Let him go,' June says all of a sudden, and the others look at her. 'If it's somethin' he needs to do, I say we let him do it.'

Glen appears doubtful. 'Does he need to do it but? Does he know what he's doin'?'

'Cross the riverbed at the jasper deposits,' Shrubb says, just as abruptly as June. 'Ya'll see them in the side of the bank. Can't miss 'em. White jasper, unlike anythin' ya've ever seen, I bet. Up the bank the other side, ya'll go across a bit of grassland and then ya'll hit the foothills. Somewhere in there.' Shrubb looks back at him now, only the slightest tremor accompanying his words. 'That's where Tobes said he was lookin'.'

Lachlan nods. 'Thanks, Shrubb.'

He's just made a move to step towards the bowsers when Pippa senses the fury burn in her throat like a rush of surprise reflux. 'Your brother wouldn't have gone out on a day like today,' she snaps. 'He wasn't that stupid. Or reckless. Not ever.'

This halts him, and for the briefest moment she thinks he might stay. But then he says, 'I'm not my brother.'

Got that right, she thinks.

And they all watch him stride away until he's gone.

Already overheating and he's only just reached the river. Mirage distorts the air a few metres ahead of him and it makes him wonder if he's hallucinating, if his brain's cooked in the boiling pot of his skull. Over fifty Shorthorn cattle roam around beside the Coongan River, must've rambled all the way over here from Limestone Station. When he stumbles towards them, they part like he's Moses or some shit. Though their dumb, glossy eyes see him as no prophet, more like he might make a race at their throats with retractable claws.

But it's no matter, Lachlan wouldn't be able to hunt a thing like this anyway, not heat-sapped, staggering for the river red gums on the grassy bank. He gulps down the last of his first two-litre water bottle, gulps too fast so some of it plumes back up into his mouth, accompanied by some bile. Looks up now to see the massive herd of cattle are directly under the enormous scarlet cliff, the landmark which gives the town its name.

Teeters for a moment, peering up at the dark spectacle of it, while the heat visibly disrupts its borders. He can see the swirls of red jasper in the big, bald face of rock.

Don't think I've ever seen anything so beautiful, he thinks in his stupor.

Once he finds the bends of white jasper in the smooth strata, like veins of vanilla in a chocolate milkshake, he ruffles down the dusty bank and into the dry riverbed, the wide trough of it completely reshaped by Shorthorn hooves. He presses through swelling waves of heat breaking against his face. Once he reaches the middle of the wide riverbed, he sees a cow watching him, similarly deranged by the fiery sky, hopelessly searching for water.

'Gorn, you!' he calls at it, as if he could pose a threat in this state. 'Git outta the river! Ya messin' it up!'

It does, galloping like a horse back up the far bank.

The unfrequented hills peer down at him as he meets the degraded bank on the other side, and Lachlan clambers up through a strange hakea garden erupting from a rubbly outcrop. The stones under his touch hot, but not hot enough to burn his skin. He has the oddest sense that if he gave up the fight, and just lay down on these rocks, they might be cool as the inside of a fridge and drink the sweat lovingly from him. These same stones might tell him everything's going to be alright. Might even tell him where his little brother got to, whisper the truth carefully into his ear.

He crosses a broiling grassland, mouthing at another water bottle. But it's scorching, warmed up already. He tries another. All of them the same: billy-can water. The only isle of shade in the flare of light is offered by a sole bloodwood tree. He leans against the trunk and chugs the hot water like he's turned the wrong handle on the kitchen tap. Lists unthinkingly, loses himself at last in the wriggle of mirage against the backlit hills. Further on, through a swipe of rising steam, crimson escarpments like Monument Valley buttes.

Stomach bloated, he keeps on. Reaches the base of the first foothill and romps it up the incline of pillow basalts. Hot, naked rocks between the spinifex and he doesn't see any legless lizards, not a single one. Wonders if it's even too hot for them to show up today.

Kissing furious sky at the peak, Lachlan nearly collapses. A shadow skips between boulders on the outcrop above, rocks black-red like they've fallen from Mars – probably some kind of marsupial – but it's retreated to cooler burrows before he can get a good look.

He's only been up here twenty minutes and he can already tell he won't last much longer. That shadow or rock wallaby he just saw, was it a shadow or rock wallaby? Or was it the essence of himself cannoned from his chest, spiralling among the outcrop burning like fire shingle?

But when he raises his head again, sweat falling from the tip of his nose like he's just clambered out of a swimming pool, he sees a pretty ravine arching above him. A ramble of rocks having tumbled down the incline, looks like it's a place where the water might rive through on those rare occasions Jasper Cliff witnesses rain.

You're losing it, Lachlan thinks when he sees a sparkle of yellow among the chert pieces.

He crouches awkwardly by a haggard sprawl of wirewood and pinches a bit of yellow out of the stone stack and he sees it's not his imagination. It is, in fact, gold. The tiniest fleck. No bigger than a mole on his chest.

'Holy shit,' Lachlan gasps, smiling.

He goes to put it in his pocket when he peers closer and sees more bits and pieces glinting among the rocky rubble. He pinches out one bit after another, until there's a tiny pile in the centre of his hand, heaped on the crimson lines of his palm. He's forced to clamber up a loose shelf, scraping a knee along the way.

'You bastard, you're going to be rich,' he says, the bizarre rush of excitement building at the base of his throat so the words are a little strained.

He drops the tiny collection of gold bits in his hand when he sees it, only because what he's collected is nothing compared to what he's looking at now, what he's discovered. As if it's just been left here for him to find, by Toby perhaps. A test, maybe? Nothing much else makes sense in this moment as the ravine throbs with astonishing, inhuman heat, down at the tiny collection of gold in his hand – but inevitable; he considers the possibility that he's imagining this. That such raging, inhuman heat has cooked his brain and there's nothing but a pile of red dirt in his palm.

The gold nugget is just a bit smaller than his hand, so when he picks it up, not all of his fingers can close around it. He's only seen gold on telly, furnaced into nice, neat bars, but this thing is ugly as hell. Staring into its cruel promise, while the foothills of the Barite Range ripple in and out of sky all about, he starts to salivate.

A clamour of everything he could do and afford. First of all, a professional to search for Toby, a PI or whatever. Only the best in the business. They'd find Toby in no time and this nightmare would be over quicker than it had begun. Then a bigger, flashier engagement ring for Shenille. He can already hear her excited squeal, the feel of her arms wrapping around his neck and the smudge of her juicy lips.

More. A nice place at Trigg, right on the beach, so he can saunter down to the shorefront cafes every morning and chill before work. Hell, he might not even need to work no more. He could show up in a Mercedes and tell Ben to jam his job where the sun definitely don't shine, and probably never has.

Even more. Nights at the casino, with Shenille, and maybe not Shenille. Other women, younger than Shenille. Lose a couple of grand on blackjack. What does it matter? There's always more where that came from.

This horny excitement only lasts as long as the gold nugget in his hand holds its terrible shine, then Lachlan's skin slowly breaks out in goosepimples. Because he turns then and sees something so beautiful – far more beautiful than the gold's shine – that he doesn't possess the words to describe it, the red hills unravelling back alongside the Coongan River, still here after slopping themselves out of the ooze when the earth was infantile. Still here, and unspoilt.

The toe he stubbed on that chain pin is no longer hurting, but now he feels the slightest throb of memory in the darkening toenail. The fist-sized nugget in his hand glistens with menace.

After all, look at what happened during the last goldrush.

He crabs it up what remains of the ravine, until he's reached the very smooth backs of the hills. From here, the view is even more stunning. The red jasper ridges arch towards higher ranges, all of it falling away, golden and sprawling, towards an unattainable horizon.

If he could just walk back to Jasper Cliff with this nugget in his hand – but the libidinous dreams have lost their kink now. He can't shake that concrete pad, that pin sticking up for anyone to stub their toe on.

Lachlan stands on the peak of the foothill, a red jasper gorge snaking below. He can't believe how lovely this land is. He pitches the nugget out into the stifling air, doesn't stay to watch where it falls.

The banter has quickly quietened down between the others, and she can see Shrubb and June staring at her with concern. She's never asked for them to watch over her, treat her like the daughter they lost thirteen years ago. Just one of those things. If she could, she'd reach into the steaming ether and yank Elizabeth back, drop her right here on the green concrete.

She chastises herself for such irresponsible whimsy, watches the low hills encircling town instead. Lachlan somewhere in the rippling ravines of it all. Toby too, perhaps.

'He'll be fine, love,' June tries to soothe her. 'Just pig-headed.'

Then Shrubb raises his eyebrows. 'Like his brother.'

'He doesn't know this place yet, that's all,' Pippa explains, rejecting their look of parental love. 'He's not ready.'

A troubled engine rumbles down the main street, and June peers at a huge Kenworth approaching, the sighing of the motor as the driver shifts gears down, slowing to 50 k's an hour as it enters town. 'Who knows?' She shrugs. 'Maybe he'll be just fine. Maybe he isn't as dumb as he looks?'

Pippa steps over to the bowsers as the semitrailer idles alongside her, the diesel fumes nearly overwhelming, the heat pitched against her from under the rig making her reel. She fuels the tank without much thought.

The tubby truckie waddles for the pub to pay, notices Glen sitting there with a Betadine-blotched bandage on his calf. 'Been in the wars, mate?'

June must've rushed inside to work the till, because the truckie comes back out, wolfing down a Corn Jack. 'We're at forty-three,' Shrubb tells the stranger as he goes. 'Already hotter than the Bar.'

'Nowhere's hotter than the Bar, buddy,' the truckie tells him, then struggles to squeeze his lard-arse back into the cab of the Kenworth.

'What a turd,' Shrubb mutters after him.

As the truck pulls away, Pippa hangs there in its contrail of diesel stink. So hot here beside the bowsers, she feels like her legs might bow under her and she could tip to the tarmac. So, what's Lachlan feeling right now, up there kissing the tops of red hills?

Two hands rest on her shoulders and she winces to feel them rasp against her skin. She knows these hands cannot belong to anything human, too lizard-like.

But when she spins around, she sees Glen up close, frowning. For the first time since she's known him, Pippa wonders what might linger behind his good humour and kindness.

'You okay, Pip?' he asks, a worried wrinkle in his brow. 'What's goin' on with you?'

Absurd, now she's really thinking about it. To believe Glen is anything but kind and caring and just a genuinely nice guy. She smiles at him, pats his reptilian hand; it's only scaly, she now sees, because of how hard he's worked his entire life. Pitted and sun-beaten.

'Nothing,' she tells him, squeezing that hand. 'I just need a walk. Clear my head.'

Her head is anything but clear as she goes down the other side of the main street and behind Aunty Belle sitting under the ghost gum. Afternoon has truly set in, and she watches the school bus trundle down Maitland Street, dropping off kids with their full schoolbags. She'd meant to walk a different way, and not end up back at the deli, but bugger it to hell, here she is. Again.

Elizabeth Shrubb stares. So too, all the other ghosts. How long will they hang onto the deli wall before the wind finally frees them, sends them down into the dead creek, covers them over with the chaff-coloured grass? How long will Aunty Belle wait for her missing daughter to come home?

Pippa thrashes away from the missing persons wall and looks down at a dead galah on the freshly watered lawn. Looks like it's simply given up in the heat and nosedived out of the ghost gum above, but now she sees it's lost most of its gaudy colouring. Been here so long it's started to turn green, and it's bloated a bit. Looks like a gross, dead pixie slowly ballooning in the forty-three-degree heat.

Pippa clips her nostrils shut with finger and thumb, so she doesn't have to smell it, and goes to step by. But the galah's beak falls open, yawning. It burps foetid air but doesn't deflate.

Its beak continues to open wider, and inside the tiny green witch, there's darkness unlike she's ever known – the inside of a kiln cooking misshaped ceramics, the door locked behind her – oppressive and somehow hotter than the scorching sky. The tiniest prick of light at its centre, and at its nexus there, is the truth.

Bright light in the darkness, as if the copper's spotlight from the other night has returned, and it carves out a scene in the pupil of this dead galah—

A Triton bundling down a lonesome road. On the way to Nullagine. The Black Range south of town, unknowable scorched hills falling away in quiet splendour.

The ute finally rattles to a halt in the gravel. The driver – none of his good humour and kindness on show. Sweat budded across his face like his skin is chill glass just removed from the fridge.

He steps from the Triton and fetches a large, crackly plastic bag. As he yanks it from the back seat, it sags heavily. Those scaly hands, hewn from hard work, clench the lip of the bag and Glen faces the Black Range. Situated here, quiet and staring, he appears darkly oracular, just him and the unknowable hills.

He walks straight out between the corkwoods, swinging the black plastic bag at his side, waving the flies on when they make a pass at his eyes. He walks for a solid couple of k's before he comes across a gully. He upturns the plastic bag and a decapitated head and two hands, lopped off at the wrists, tumble out.

A face filmed with dust after rolling into the gully.

'Nothin' personal, Shrubby,' Glen says.

Pippa stomps on the fat bird, as if to break its awful spell, because she doesn't want to see anymore. Doesn't want to *know* anymore. And just like that, she can't remember how she got here.

Whenever she tries to fetch back the dream, it sluices off her skin like tap water running between her fingers. Something about the Black Range maybe? South of town here? A car on a road? No, it's all gone. Nothing now.

She looks down and sees her rubber thong buried in the chest of a dead galah and she groans with the reek. Hurries away and looks around.

All as it should be in Jasper Cliff. Aunty Belle under her tree, waiting. June and Shrubb sitting on the pub verandah.

And Glen.

Glen there too, and he's scratching at that bandage on his calf.

She's been meaning to ask what he's gone and done to himself. She'll have to keep an eye on the silly old bugger. After all, he's no spring chicken anymore.

A surprising, triumphant return. Stumbling back towards the pub right on dark, Jasper Cliff weirdos hoot and cheer. Say, 'Thank God you're alive.' 'Knew ya had it in ya.' 'Tough as fucken nails, aren't ya?'

There's slaps and pats on the back. Pippa brings out the cheese kranskys and mushroom pies which didn't sell at the servo today, or any day. Lachlan eats and listens to them laugh and he reckons Glen might be right.

This place is growing on him after all.

The ravine of exposed basalts has cooled long before the baking tops of hills far above it, and at its furthest reaches – across which garlands of red jasper are wound through the rock – is that place the whitefellas call the Rift. A wizened crack up through glabrous red stone. The hint of an animal's eye glimpsed deep within.

Lachlan tramped within metres of its edge only hours earlier but had been so frazzled by the grandeur of these hills, he had failed to glance down and find the prize his little brother had been searching for.

At the mouth of the ravine is a wretched puddle of rainwater, favoured by the wildlife, but it has begun to fester, spoilt by the carcass of a Shorthorn calf lounging half in the cesspool and half on the bank, its coat a sloppy dressing for its clean bones. Only the Rift witnessed the calf's demise. None other had seen, nor cared, how it extinguished and came to foul the water.

The thing concealed within the Rift knows many things. It sees further, into all the cracks in the chert hills, as far away as the Black Range, and back through time too, to a place where white men or sometimes Chinese prospectors met the earth's remonstrance as their mines steadily filled with carbon monoxide, leaving a handful gasping, and then dead. It also knows what happened to Toby Bowman, on what plain he now lies.

But who should it show the truth to when no one has stumbled down the ravine in so long, seeking it out?

7

The whole town is caught in a perpetual state of waiting, the humans sweating and sometimes silent on the verandah of the pub, which isn't really a pub anymore. And the critters too. Lachlan only notices this when Shrubb jumps from his chair, knocking it over.

'What is it, dickhead?' Glen blurts, stamps a hand over his heart. 'Almost gave me a bloody stroke.'

Pippa and June are chatting in the corner, so haven't reacted to this, to the clap, clap of Shrubb's thongs pursuing whatever he just caught sight of. Lachlan does start a little, but only because he was glaring out at the warm curvatures of the Barite Range encircling town. After yesterday's expedition, he's already shivering with anticipation to get back out there.

Glen looks at Lachlan, shakes his head. 'I swear there's not a brain between those ears sometimes.'

But when Lachlan follows Shrubb out into the blaze of day – the sky's spotlight burning down on the two men, on them but also everywhere else at once – he sees a red-faced lizard squatting on the roasting footpath. Shrubb's got a ridiculous smile mortared across his face, kneeling to get a better look at the little dragon.

While they all wait, each beset by their own private hopes and fears, the lizard waits for the sun to get higher, hotter, so it can marinate itself in all that ferocious energy.

Now Lachlan's kneeling too, Shrubb turns to him. 'They reckon lizards can see so much more than us people, eh? Saw it on ABC the other night.' The Burton's legless lizard cocks its head back at them, cute as a scaly Labrador. 'Can't remember exactly how it goes, but it's like we've only got three of these sorta receptors in our eyes, while lizards have more.' He points up. 'See that sun's puttin' out a bloody rainbow of shit we have no idea about. We can only see some of it.' Then he nods back down at the red-faced lizard. 'But this little bugger. He can see it *all.* So much more than we could ever hope to. He can just see to the truth of things.' Shrubb shakes his head in astonishment, and Lachlan grins at him, at the wonder in his voice. 'Would come in handy every now and then, eh?'

Shrubb chuckles to himself, but when he reaches out a finger to brush along the rough capping of the lizard's head, it blasts away under the gate beside the pub.

Just as Shrubb says this, Lachlan peers back down the main street and watches the police paddy wagon roll slowly into town. While he's been waiting for the buggers to show for days now, he can't help but feel a stab of disappointment – that he won't be able to return to the foothills near the Coongan River as quickly as he'd first hoped.

He stands, bedraggled, clothes soaked with sweat. 'Visitors,' Lachlan says.

Shrubb sees the paddy wagon and, as quick as the lizard, he vaults the gate and there's a loud thudding the other side, the hurried clap, clapping of his thongs against the soles of his hardened feet. Lachlan stares at the gate for a moment, then pisses himself laughing.

He looks back at June who's now standing in the hot light watching. 'I'd never be able to run in thongs,' Lachlan tells her.

'Told ya,' she says, tracking the wagon's approach too now. 'Parkin' fines.'

Pippa and Glen nod to the two police officers who pull up right alongside the pub, blocking the view of town. The man who slides out of the driver's side looks like he's just left high school, thumbs hooked in his shiny high-vis vest. His youth only serves to douse Lachlan in further dread, especially when he sees the young bloke has nicked himself shaving this morning, just the tiniest point of dried blood on his chin.

A young woman about the same age steps out the passenger side and the driver's eyes roam across them all before settling on June. 'Aunty,' he says.

'Ryan Connor,' without a smile. 'If we knew ya were comin' today, we woulda shouted ya a homecomin' party. Rolled out the red bloody carpet.'

He smiles at that. The other police officer joins his side now and she quivers on the spot like she might faint at any moment. She's only been out of the aircon for seconds. Pippa hands her a little bottle of water.

'We're here to speak to Lachlan Bowman.'

Lachlan steps back into the shade of the pub and goes to open his mouth, when June cuts in, 'Belle's just down the road there, son. Got anythin' to say to her while ya here? Reckon ya may as well, since ya've driven all the way out here from the Bar. Any news on her daughter yet, Ryan?'

Connor's head turns slow and deliberate like someone palming at a pale blue desk globe. He peers down at the patient shape of Aunty Belle under the rustling ghost gum.

'She waits there every day, ya know?' June persists. 'Or maybe ya don't know? Maybe ya'd know if ya dropped round ya hometown more often, eh? Visited ya mob every now and then?'

Now Glen pipes up. 'Was that you two the other night?' He scratches at his bandage. 'With the spotlight?' Looks at June. 'See, yeah, he visits. He was here shinin' that big bloody spotlight into his own people's houses the other night.'

'Think that might've been the sarge, actually.' Connor says and pushes up his sunnies. His eyes swivel, patient and dark, and finally fix on Lachlan, the only unfamiliar face here on the hot verandah. 'Bowman?' he asks.

Lachlan nods.

'Go have a word with Belle while ya here, eh?' June continues. 'Maybe just give her an update on how the investigation's goin'? What leads ya got? Anythin' like that?'

Lachlan senses himself shrink in the face of all this tension. Connor remains unbothered, drinking in his hometown, while surely there's a drumhead trial happening right here and now, and the young bloke's bound to get hung, drawn and quartered.

'Step inside?' Connor asks him, then glances at Pippa. 'That suitable?'

She nods, and at least she spares him a smile, faint as it is.

They sit at the bar and the constable takes his statement while Connor walks around querulously, as if checking the pub over for possible code violations. It's only about halfway through that Lachlan realises Connor's listening intently, just trying not to look like he is. The constable is the kind of chick he might've hit on before he met Shenille. She stepped fresh from the paddy wagon with her puffy pink lips and platinum hair pulled back in a ponytail, but after just twenty minutes inside, she's caked in perspiration and her skin's turned ashen.

'Any news?' he asks her, then glances at Connor, who's now staring at a series of framed black-and-white photographs of five constables posturing in front of the Ripon Hills during the goldrush, uniforms and rifles on display with terrible pride. 'On Toby?'

'When your mother made the initial report, a statewide description of his vehicle went out,' the constable explains, then tries for a reassuring expression, despite her obvious suffering. 'We'll find him. Don't worry.'

'Raeside,' Connor mutters from the corner of the pub, a warning in his tone.

Her timbre shifts slightly. 'We're doing everything we can to find him.'

'Are you guys going to check the hills here? Near the river? Like I said, he was looking for something up there.'

'Like what?' Connor smirks, turning back to look at them. 'Gold?'

A flash of that nugget he pitched into the gorge yesterday, wondering if he'd imagined the whole thing. Dreamed it into blue sky. Because now when he tries to draw back in the memory of that big golden chunk, he can only visualise himself holding a piece of red chert – no different to the countless others filling the creek bed – just before he lobbed it.

Fear trickles through his nervous system to see the lack of

feeling on Connor's face. In those eyes brimming with disregard, Lachlan sees he must become like everyone else in Jasper Cliff, obsequious and quiet. He must learn to wait, like Aunty Belle. Sit under the tree and stare down the street all day and wonder what might manifest from the sprawl of mirage year after year after year.

Constable Raeside stares daggers at him now, then turns back to Lachlan. 'It does seem unlikely he would still be in this area.'

'Why's that?' Lachlan snaps a bit too harshly.

'He took his vehicle. If it was still around town somewhere, or even along the Coongan River, someone would've found it by now. Idle cars don't last very long out this way. There are entire FIFO crews dedicated to going out on the roads to strip broken-down cars for parts. A whole black market for that stuff runs out of the mines.'

Lachlan nods, can't meet the false hope in her eyes any longer. *Doesn't mean I'm going to stop looking.*

'So what does that leave us with now?' he asks.

'Well, we've checked with all the nursing stations in the surrounding towns, Marble Bar and Nullagine, and there's been no sign of him,' Connor tells him quietly, finally meeting his eyes in the dim of the pub. 'He hasn't been admitted to any of the hospitals along the coast, so that's a good thing when you think about it.'

Lachlan nods. 'That's the good news, yeah. But I can tell there's some bad news, too.'

'He hasn't used his mobile phone,' Raeside breaks it to him softly, glancing back at Connor. 'That's the bad news. Not since the night of October seventeenth. And he hasn't accessed any of his bank accounts.' She must note the instant dismay on his face because she inches a little closer but remains careful not to intrude on his personal space. 'That doesn't mean worst-case scenario. It just means we need to keep looking. There are things you can do, you and your mum. Like put out the word on Facebook. Stuff like that.'

'I'm not on Facebook,' Lachlan says. Then realises how ungrateful this must sound. He smiles at Raeside. 'But what the hell? I guess it's about time I joined.'

'Why so long to report him missing?' Connor asks now, striding over and placing his cap down on the bar top.

Lachlan stares at the dark halo of sweat above the cap's visor. 'I knew he was here. Said he was researching his novel. He was a bit of a budding writer. But we only called each other once every fortnight, something like that. Sometimes it was longer between calls.'

'So you two weren't super close then?' Connor glances at Raeside, but she looks a bit pissed with him now.

'We were close.'

'Not close enough to tell you where he might be headed next?'

He'd felt bad for Connor back out on the verandah, with June and Glen tearing shreds off him; now Lachlan wishes they'd torn into him more. 'It's been a busy year for me,' he explains quietly, resolve shattered. 'Toby was moving around a lot. Hanging around Cue at first and then coming up here. Half the time he didn't even have reception. When he did call Mum and I, he did it from payphones most of the time. I suppose, I also had a lot going on. I got engaged, moved in with my fiancée.'

'Congratulations,' Constable Raeside adds.

'So, too busy to check up on your little brother?'

Lachlan glares at him, grinding his teeth. Can see the pink scratchy lines on Connor's chin where he misjudged the angle of his razor. 'We done now?'

Connor turns away. 'Send Pippa in, thanks.'

Somehow, it's easier to breathe back outside, the light intense but at least the heat isn't trapped and festering, like it was back at the bar. He nods at Pippa, 'They want to have a word,' he tells her. 'But just watch out for that Connor bloke. He won't be in charge of public relations anytime soon.'

She appears to only half hear this, floating past him with a distant look in her eyes.

'How'd it go?' Glen asks, no hope in his voice.

Lachlan shakes his head. 'Don't ask.'

Connor and Raeside interview all of them, leaving Glen for last. He's been expecting this day to come for a decade now. Since he bashed Muswell's skull in so much it changed shape, folded inward and dispelled Muswell's fat, blue tongue from his mouth, which hung out like a discoloured snail trying to escape its broken shell.

The memory leaves him tingling, light-headed with joy.

Glen sits on the bar stool and they ask him question after question but every question is about Toby. What did Toby say, what was he like the day before he left, did he see Toby and Pippa ever arguing? They don't utter Ricky Muswell's name, not once. And how can they truly not know? How can he have spent the last ten years waiting to be judged for such a thing and no punishment ever arrive?

You really don't have a clue, do ya?

Glen watches Connor, the young cop turning to survey the inside of the pub again, not waiting for or caring about the answer.

Ten years since he was tasked with walking out into the wirewood on his own. He and Muswell had stayed in contact over the radio but by the end of the third day, he noticed the dumb little bastard hadn't called with his three o'clock check-in. Not too worried at first, Glen set up in the shade of some Cole's wattles and snoozed – too knackered to bother setting up the tent – feeling about as Zen as he'd ever felt in his life.

Under the rustle of wattle leaves, he recalled how Layla used to go on and on about that. How her much younger, yoga instructor was the only one who could get her to that pure place of Zen. Yeah, he was giving her *Zen*, alright. Giving it to her five times a week as it turned out.

'Fuckers,' Glen muttered aloud, and then laughed. Because out there all his problems seemed so far away, without substance. Microscopic in comparison to the jaggy lines of hills falling away in every direction.

He tried to radio Muswell a couple more times into the night and, while he still wasn't particularly concerned, decided it best to contact base once it got to nine pm and tried not to sound too flippant. They said they'd send a vehicle out to search for Muswell first thing in the morning but could Glen also set out at dawn, cut across the spinifex to the east and meet up with the opposing boundary fence, just in case Muswell happened to be somewhere in that vicinity. Made sense, considering there was a water tank somewhere around the ten-k mark.

Dumb prick, Glen remembers thinking. *Not stuck listening to the little shit natter anymore but he's still ruinin' my good time.*

Glen did as instructed the following morning, set off east across the hummock grassland, through groves of mulga so leafless it looked like they'd been hit with some kind of defoliant – he wouldn't have put that past the mining company either. He shooed on the Shorthorn calves which took off like huge, frightened puppies when they saw him draw near. Then after a while, he didn't think this was so bad after all. Not as he started scrambling his way up low hills thick with conkerberry, the caudle of blue sky funnelled straight into his mouth, and he supped and supped until he felt bloated and wonderfully alien inside his own skin.

Zen, mate. Just fucken Zen.

Reached the eastern boundary fence around two in the afternoon and took to the shade below a batswing coral tree. Forty-two degrees that day, though it felt closer to forty-four, and he was going silly with delight, or heatstroke; hard to tell the difference. He tried Muswell on the radio twice with no success, then radioed base to report his arrival. The search vehicle hadn't seen Muswell either, yet.

He'd just flumped back against the trunk of the coral tree to shovel a can of lemon and pepper tuna into his gob with a plastic spoon, fending off the eager flies, when he looked up at the rocky fold of a hill just a few metres away. The spoon, heaped with pinky mush, hovered before his open mouth as he watched the auburn shape scamper away. The white spots along its back lingered before his eyes.

It was the size of a rabbit, and about as fast as one, and

Glen only saw it for a split second, but he knew what it was. Ridiculously excited, he took out the GPS and wrote down the coordinates in his notepad. Beside it, his shaky writing hand scratched out the word: *Quoll!!*

Muswell came staggering down the fence line about an hour later. Glen peered up at him with a lack of surprise, too high on the grasslands he'd traversed to get here, and the quoll sighting, to really care much. About two hundred metres away, fencing materials were neatly stacked and Muswell was so zapped, he tripped on a roll of grey wire, knocked a long star picket out of the heap.

'What took ya so long?' Glen asked once he reached the shade of the tree.

'Water!' Muswell bawled, demanding as a six-year-old who's only ever got what he always wanted.

'Where's ya radio? Ya backpack?'

'Fucken lost 'em, okay? I lost it all, Bubs. Just gimme a bloody drink or I'm gunna cark it right here and now. Askin' me stupid questions when I'm dyin' of thirst here.'

Just like that, Glen's good mood was torn from him. The best he'd felt in decades, spoilt by this selfish, ginger-mulleted turd. Hadn't felt this good since he was a kid. Those times he stole away behind the shed with a neighbour's cat, with a mouse he snatched from under the fridge.

Watching Muswell chug at a bottle, he had to repress the urge to remind the young man there was a water tank at the ten-k mark along the eastern boundary – and if he'd stuck to the fence he would've surely seen it.

'Saw a quoll,' he told Muswell, not able to contain his excitement any longer. Then pointed to the hill. 'Just over there.'

'Fuck's that?'

'Havin' me on, aren't ya? It's one of the things we're sposed to be out here lookin' for. A rare marsupial. Not sposed to be hardly any left up this way. But I saw one. Took down the coordinates so they can send scientists back out and that.'

He made the mistake of showing Muswell the hand-scrawled numbers on his notepad. Muswell peered down at this, drank some more. Then, without a flinch, Muswell tore the page away. Glen was too shocked to make a sound, watching the pieces scatter into the spinifex.

'You're a dumb old bastard,' Muswell told him matter-of-factly. 'The company doesn't *want* us to find anythin'. Didn't ya get that? They *need* to be seen to look for rare and endangered shit. Just as long as we don't find none. Jeezus, why do I have to spell that out to ya?'

'But I – I did,' Glen stuttered. 'I found the quoll.'

'I didn't see it. How sure are ya?' He drank more from Glen's water bottle. 'Ninety percent sure? Seventy-five?' Dry lips now shiny with drink. 'Doesn't matter anyway. If ya report somethin' like that, it could shut the whole operation down. Millions of fucken dollars, Bubs. Even if ya make the report – which I don't suggest ya do – it's not gunna stop 'em in the long run. Just means they'll spend thousands in legal costs and the thing'll get delayed for a few years.' He laughs. 'Then how happy ya reckon they'll be with ya? And I'm sure-as-shit not gunna back ya up. After all, I wanna get paid.' He raised his feral, ratty eyebrows. 'Don't you?'

Glen's lips firmed. 'I know what I saw.' Then shrugged a little stiffly. 'I'm not gunna lie about it.'

'Oh yeah, coz you've got the eyesight of a man half ya age, I'm bettin.' Muswell laughed harder. 'When was the last time ya had them tested, Bubs?'

'Stop callin' me that.'

'I need more water.' He dropped the bottle he just finished, held out his hand. 'Chop-chop. Quick as ya can.'

Glen handed him another. 'I don't care what ya say when we get back. I'm gunna tell them the truth.'

Muswell watched him over the lip of the bottle as he kept chugging, a sly glint in his obdurate eyes. Then he finished, wiped his mouth on the back of his hand. 'And I'll tell them you're a bullshit artist. I'll say ya told me ya made the sightin' up coz ya secretly a greenie and ya don't want the project to go ahead.' Raised his thin eyebrows again. 'How's that sound?'

Trembling head to toe, Glen found himself floating away, out from under the shadow of the batswing coral tree. *Zen, remember?* But even his internal voice was becoming increasingly obscured by whatever this thing was rising in him blackly. *Don't get angry, mate. Stay Zen. Just fucken Zen.*

'Actually, maybe we should go over there and smash the little thing's head in?' Muswell called after him, then gargled on more of Glen's water. 'That way no bastard will ever find it.'

A flash of mice and neighbourhood cats he did away with when he was a kid, how he fizzed with the thrill of listening to their cries thin out into nothing. Peering up at the quiver of spinifex, gilt and stretching in every direction, he imagined the quoll in his tightening grip, but could only feel his hands relaxing, awestruck.

Glen searched the fence wire and the answer presented itself at his feet. The long star picket Muswell had kicked from the pile of equipment. When Glen floated down towards it, saw himself wrap his fingers around its dusty length, it felt so right in his hand. When he turned back, the spiky orange-red pea flowers in the tree above Muswell glowed with hectic colour, fierce as fire coral.

The flowers glowed hotter each time the star picket connected with the back of Muswell's head, each time a spatter of blood dotted the wedge-shaped leaflets. And the spinifex grasslands were more than alive; pulsating like a massive heart just hit with the defib. Glen soaked up their strange energy, hitting Muswell again, and this time saw how his front teeth caved inwards and probably rattled against the back of his throat.

Glen blinks, starting to find it's ten years later and the two cops are standing right in front of him. He watches Raeside finish writing in her notepad and imagines she's taking his confession.

To this day, no one has found Muswell's body. Despite Glen hastily dragging him off into the spinifex, digging a hole with his camp shovel and covering the little bastard back over with crimson sand.

The search had predominantly focused on where they found Muswell's backpack and radio, about seven k's down the fence line.

When Glen got back to the mine, he reported his sighting of the quoll. Gave them the GPS coordinates after jotting them down a second time. Then he also emailed those coordinates to the Department of Water and Environmental Regulation. Just in case Muswell was right about the mining company's intentions to bury any possible sightings of rare fauna.

Raeside snaps her notepad shut, smiles at him. 'Right, I think that's everything, Glen. Thanks for your help.' Lets her pen rest on the bar top. 'As long as there isn't anything else you wanted to add?'

Glen returns her smile and shakes his head slowly. 'Nup,' he says. 'Can't think of anythin'.'

A chill in the air now, despite it being over forty-three, as Lachlan watches Connor and Raeside step back out onto the verandah. June has her back turned to them, glaring into the unseen, and has been for some time. A couple of times Glen has touched her shoulder and whispered sweet comforts.

Connor's sight roves across all gathered there, fixes on Lachlan. 'We'll be in touch if there's any news. With you and your mother.' He pulls his cap back on, still dark with perspiration. Then looks at Pippa. 'In the meantime, if any of you hear from Toby. Just give us a bell.'

'Thanks again,' Raeside tries for a wan smile.

'What happens now?' Pippa asks, voice slightly choked. 'I meant to ask back inside.'

Raeside opens her mouth to speak, but Connor cuts her off. 'A description of his vehicle has gone out statewide, so I'd hope that yields some results soon.'

'You hope?' June snaps. 'What good is hope in this place?'

Connor refuses to meet June's eyes; Lachlan realises he hasn't done the whole time he's been here. 'We can only do what we can.'

'I guess what worries me is how ya decide to spend ya time, that's all. Like showin' up here at eight o'clock to shut down a party at the Neave house, when ya could be out there lookin' for Tobes.'

'I told you, that wasn't us.'

'Or some other poor bugger who's in trouble.'

She points down the road and Lachlan's surprised by the gust of Language which streams from her. Lachlan twists his neck to peer down at the ghost gum, Aunty Belle patiently staring at the parked paddy wagon. Connor speaks softly, says something back in Language; the argument continuing though no one else on the verandah can understand what's being said.

'And what about my Liz?' June jabs her finger in the hot air. As soon as she says this, Lachlan watches Glen and Pippa bristle. 'Ten years, Ryan. Ten-fucken-years.'

Connor says something more in Language. Hearing it spoken aloud is like listening to the hot wind wending across the Barite Range, a thing so inexplicably beautiful Lachlan brims with feeling.

Now June lowers her head, thumbs at her brow. 'I don't lay it all at your feet, son. I don't know what it's like to put that God-awful uniform on every morning. But how long is this place gunna wait for the truth? You were our great and shinin' hope, ya know that? When ya went away to the academy in the big smoke, when ya graduated, we were all here dancin' in the bloody streets. *These* bloody streets.'

Lachlan tries to imagine what it's been like for Connor since he left Jasper Cliff. Trying to change an institution like the Western Australian Police Force from the inside out. He could imagine it wouldn't take long to burn out, feel crushed to a fine powder.

The expectations of an entire town. So many people who have lost so much already.

Connor has lowered his head too, while June rages. Now his chin tilts and he finally meets her sad eyes. 'There has to be something left behind,' he tells her quietly. 'In order to follow the trail, there has to be some trace to lead us in the right direction.' He glances down towards Belle. 'I'm not overstating it in saying, there's nothing, Aunty June. There's nothing.'

'There's us,' she tells him. 'We're what's left behind.'

But is that enough? Lachlan senses the mind-boggling heat wrap around them all here on the verandah, the patient and the watchful, what remains of the lost.

Connor looks at Lachlan one last time. 'We'll be in touch,' he says.

Lachlan wonders if that's true, watching Connor and Raeside return to their paddy wagon. He sees June's turned away again, not sure if she's hiding her tears from the rest of them. The paddy wagon grumbles back to life and they hear the aircon kick in. It drives right by Aunty Belle, then out the other side of town again. Like they were never really here, figments of imagination. Ghosts.

He watches them go, carrying the last of his hope on their tailwind. But then they're gone too. Lost.

Glen sees the moment her resolve breaks, and he's up and out of his camp chair, flinging an arm around Pippa's shoulders. Been watching it swell in her these past few days, since Lachlan showed up, the dread like a bucket left under a running tap; now the water's spilling over the brim and flooding the pavement.

She butts her face straight into his chest and weeps, and he smooths back her straw-coloured hair and tells her it'll all be alright. Even as he has no idea if that's true or not. He knows *he* didn't hurt Toby, not like he did Muswell. He liked Toby a lot, as much as he likes Lachlan. Didn't mean it was all going to work out fine. Didn't mean some other mean bastard out there, just like Glen, didn't get his grubby mitts on the young bloke.

Ricky Muswell's family must've surely gone through this. The worry building in them until they broke down and cried and swore and bashed their fists against the ground with the injustice of it all. Wishing the little ginger fuck back home safe and sound.

Didn't mean it was going to happen.

Glen watches the paddy wagon disappear in the sloshy distance, mirage unfolding over town. After he'd buried Muswell, he'd just started to walk. Walked and walked in the dusk with the blood still stuck to his skin, until he felt it dry and go tight, and all the chert outcrops shone, spearing him with their light. Certain he forfeited something that day, the last vestiges of his humanity, and it was a trade he would've made long ago, if only he'd known. The clarity of this. This and him, united. He just had to bash someone's brains out to see it.

'Fuck, sorry, Glen,' she says into his chest, but won't let go.

So he hugs her tighter, Pippa's arms thin as spindles around him. 'Got nothin' to be sorry about, my lovely. They'll find him. They're not all completely useless. And in the meantime, I'm not goin' anywhere. Not me or June or Shrubby.' Then meets Lachlan's eyes. Lachlan nods back. 'Or Lachie for that matter.'

So long since a woman pressed up against him, he wonders what he's truly capable of. To do something as audacious as what he did to Muswell and never be judged for it surely made him bulletproof. And he'll do it again, Glen understands that so fully in this moment. And it'll have to be someone here – someone he has easy access to – despite him really enjoying the company of them all. Maybe even loving them, in his own away. But it just made sense to choose someone close. In waiting for the lost, they're all halfway lost themselves. He just needed to give them that last little shove in the back.

It's nothing personal.

He might draw it out next time – make his heady union with the dirt and rocks and trees last longer. He might pick Pippa and take his fill of her first, really make her beg for him to hurt her a little less, before he reaches for the star picket.

Looking at Pippa in his arms, he realises how much like Hannah Parslow she is, the last true friend he ever had. Her milk-pale British skin, her hair the colour of wheat. She's like Hannah, just all grown up and filled out. Back when he showed Hannah into the shed decades ago, he'd felt no inclination to hurt her.

Glen shuts his eyes now, stroking her hair ever so softly. If his chest could yaw open like a hatch, and if Pippa were permitted to see inside, would she turn away so definitely as Hannah had? Would she turn and run as fast as she could?

8

Lachlan can't just sit here and wait for nothing to drive down that road, for one of the vanished to come sauntering along the gravel shoulder, waving a hand out like they haven't been missing all these years.

So less than fifteen minutes after the paddy wagon has gone, Lachlan fetches his backpack and hunches by the fridge behind the bar, filling it with three water bottles and a couple of Mars bars – all he'll need under the scalding sky.

Shrubb has just slinked back from the side of the pub as Lachlan steps out into the hard light. 'What I miss?' he asks.

'Not a whole lot,' Lachlan tells him, already crossing the scorched road.

'Jeez, you took off in a hurry,' Glen tells Shrubb. 'Ya can move when ya bloody want to, can't ya? Like a fat kid to a free lunch.'

Lachlan doesn't glance back to check on them, can only feel them go quiet now he's setting off. Their hopeful eyes following as he goes. This time they don't call out, summon him back. They understand why he's headed back to the foothills by the river, what he's looking for.

The cattle from Limestone Station are back by the Coongan River. One calf bolts away at the sight of him and he grimaces at its shit-caked tail flapping behind it. They list uselessly in the roaring sunlight, some drooling bucketloads, too dimwitted to seek shelter below the river red gums.

Most appear unperturbed by his return, too heat-whacked to care perhaps, and Lachlan crosses down into the riverbed, scrambling through roots half dead and showing through crumbly loam. He's about halfway across, crunching over this dark crust of earth, like the burning surface of Mars under his feet, when he sees a lemonade can crushed into the dirt. He reaches down without thinking to collect it and as soon as he touches the aluminium, the dented surface burns his fingertips, having absorbed the unimaginable heat. He barks, puts his fingers in his mouth. Wraps the can in his snake bandage instead, deposits it into his pack to bin when he gets back to the Cliff.

The light glares off black rock. Light can be refashioned here, jumps back off the pumice-like surface with a very different kind of shine to it, stark and piercing his eyes. Immured by ravine walls, he lists in a snag of corkwoods and conkerberry, and realises he doesn't even know what the Rift looks like. Wouldn't know the fucking thing even if he saw it. His brain twitches inside the hotpot of his skull. Maybe he's never been looking for Toby at all. More like he's asked something of these foothills – some unanswerable question – and now he's just hanging around ridiculously, waiting.

He sits there for most of the day, seeking a reply from the mouthless stones. The shade keeps the punishing sun off his skin but still his mind goes grey. Once afternoon's scrubbed the blue from the sky, Lachlan forces himself to move on. And as soon as he's halfway up the next incline, he peers back to find a speechless sect of euros watching him from the low hummock grassland. He wonders if they've been there all that time, just beyond view, silent as he despaired in the shade of trees.

He trudges back to town in the dusk, waves of heat peeling back off the bitumen. The mood no less dire when he reaches the verandah. June and Shrubb and Glen sipping lemonade, Pippa leaning in the doorway. Hours have been and gone and the congress stand gathered as if he was never gone at all. They need not ask him a thing as he's returned from the Coongan River alone again. Found nothing and returned with less. Only the crushed can of lemonade he drops in the bin without comment.

He waits till later that night, his shirt stiff as plasterboard with old sweat. Watches Shrubb drift away, then June. Off into the quiet of the night streets. He can't help but remember that mob of euros just before he left the foothills, immovable in their vigil. Thinks of how they mobbed together – even as he watches the little verandah family gently break apart like a biscuit dropped into warm milk.

As soon as he can be sure the old pub pipes won't flay the skin from his back, Lachlan makes for the communal bathroom. He turns the tap and quickly withdraws his hand in case the water is still boiling. It's not, allows him to step in. Lovely and cool. The cold rush trying to strip the pink heat rash from his skin.

He listens to someone shuffle into the cubicle beside him, the shower spray, and then a body thudding in under the stream. Hangs there a moment longer in disbelief, wondering if one of the old Jasper Cliff ghosts has wandered in from the outside.

'Who's that?' Lachlan calls out, an exhausted twinge in his voice.

'Who's fucken *that*?' The voice calls back, outraged. 'It's me, dumb-dumb.' A smile in Glen's tone, salving to hear it after the bugger of today. Reassuring as the cold water encasing Lachlan's stubbornly overheated body.

Lachlan's words hang back in his throat a spell before he asks, 'What are you doing?'

'What's it sound like? I'm havin' a bloody wash.'

'Why here, though? Got a home, don't you?'

'The water's out at my joint. Useless bloody shire,' he calls above the partition. 'Pip lets me have a scrub 'ere when I need to. What is this, twenty questions? Go about ya business.'

Only the running water of the showers for a spell, then there's a huge, wet fart in the cubicle next door to Lachlan. The sound of it so loud it ricochets off the tiled walls.

'Ya hear that ripper?'

Lachlan doesn't know what to say, the cold water whacking all the raw patches of his sunburn.

'Ya heard it, ya dirty perv,' Glen chuckles.

With that, Lachlan starts to laugh hysterically. Glen laughs back, but then a fetid stink fills the cubicle and Lachlan gags. 'Ah! You bastard!'

'Breathe deep, son! Breathe deep!'

Having escaped Glen's fart, he quickly wraps himself in his towel and finds it so hot on the rack it feels like it's just been put through the dryer. Freshly dressed and smelling like roses and making sluggishly for his room, he peers out at the verandah to see Pippa's the only one to remain this late in the night – apart from Glen still singing that Midnight Oil song about the bullroarer in the shower – and she's keeping vigil over Jasper Cliff. Seeing her from behind like this, beams of moonlight flush against her flanks, she looks very much like Aunty Belle, has that same stiff patience.

If Lachlan had never shown up in town, she would've never known Toby was missing. She could've lived with the lie that Toby had done a runner on her – painful as that scenario was – and he'd shacked up with some younger chick in some other deadbeat town half cooked to death. Just another arsehole who'd tricked her into thinking she was loved.

He spends day after searing day like this, weeks even – difficult to tell without much structure to the hours. He gets up and hangs around on the verandah with the others a while before fetching his pack and setting off for the river. In the foothills, sometimes the Burton's legless lizards scamper to the top of a boulder and cock a thoughtful eye at him. Lachlan halts in his tracks through the weird hakeas to watch them back, and recalls what Shrubb said about reptiles being able to see so much more of the world than humankind. Being able to see straight to the core of things in a way people can never hope to. Can they see ribboning bands of UV, a whole spectrum of colours caking over the river and foothills like another language written upon the sky, looping runes which would boggle the human mind?

But how much further can those eyes see? Can they also perforate the walls of time and witness what happened to Toby? The terrible and inescapable truth of what has happened to his little brother?

Lachlan flinches as a falcon zips down and snatches the lizard off the rock right in front of him. It's jolting to have their eye contact broken so cruelly. He blinks at how quickly the lizard has vanished. 'Didn't see that coming but, did you?' he mutters.

He's just turned back for the bank when there's a loud hissing at his foot. Lachlan leaps away, certain there's some mean python in the grass about to strike. But it's only a shred of black plastic bag, torn on the corkwoods in the wind and snaking around in the grass below, the breeze sliding through and making the plastic hiss. He unravels it, looping it around one hand, and takes the bag with him. By the time he's back in the riverbed, the pack hanging onto his shoulders is crammed with litter he's collected from the foothills, washed or blown out of the streets of town.

Almost completely robbed of energy, he staggers the rest of the way back to the Cliff but not even the exhaustion can maim his delight at sunset, how the hills follow at one side, curved below a marooning sky.

He can already see this place has changed the design of his life. Once Toby is found safe and well – *and he will be*, he has to remind himself over and over – Lachlan can finally quit his job in the city. Might take some convincing Shenille but she could easily get a job at the East Pilbara Shire with her qualifications. A sting of doubt to think of how beachy she is, but the nearest beach is only two hours away. She might be okay with that. He can only hope.

He could get some dead-end job here in town too and dedicate the rest of his time to these hills by the river, keep them safe, keep them free of human debris. Spend his days trawling for litter and jamming it into his backpack. Sure, it's a losing battle. A mug's game. There'd always be more crap left around by people, as long as there's people. He wishes he could just do away with the people but he can't so he'll just clean up after them. He'll scrounge around and try to fix the damage they leave behind. He'll keep those foothills clean and safe. He'll hide the cricket ball–sized nuggets of gold wherever he finds them.

Every night he arrives back at Pippa's pub lifts him higher than the last, this strange congress waiting for him on the warm concrete. Each time they seem even gladder he's returned, that he's survived another day out there in the unimaginable heat. Shenille, on the other hand, sounds like she's losing patience when he calls her on June's mobile to recount effusively the wonders he's seen up in the foothills. Every night, she seems further disinterested, asks him when he'll be coming home.

After the latest call, he finds himself drifting back out onto the verandah, shoeless, and hoping his bare, pallid feet don't reek, before listing lazily in his camp chair. Not even Shenille's increasing indifference can bring him down while he has the whole, cluttered, ramble of the little town at his feet, ramshackle as the design of the chert and basalt hills back along the river.

His cheery mood is only ever harpooned when the family inevitably breaks up, as it does around the same time every night. Usually they peer down the road sometime after dark to find Aunty Belle has snuck off without anyone noticing. Then Shrubb drifts away from the pub, singing out his goodbyes. This is closely followed by June, as if she's perpetually got her eye on the silly bugger, making sure he doesn't come to any harm. Finally Glen, making a bad joke or two, before disappearing into the gloom in front of the old bakery.

Pippa is always left standing on the verandah, watching over the Cliff. Lachlan would like to linger one time, stay as long as she does under the watchful moon, but he's usually driven inside by the prospect of a cold shower, if only to wash the sticky sweat from his skin.

Lachlan is the first to stir and wander outside the next morning. His feet bare and expecting the flakily painted concrete to be cool under his soles, it's already a hotplate slowly warming up, even at half-six in the morning.

The town greets him, rubbing its tin backs against the sky. But his attention is drawn harder by the Barite Range, already fantasising about being back out there, surrounded by curios of stone.

He thinks that in searching for his little brother, he's found something he never thought possible. Something to dedicate his life to.

Lachlan shuts his eyes to draw in the barren surface of the wide empty river, the eyes of the Burton's legless lizard, the mob of scarlet euros closing ranks around him, when his nostrils flare, sniff. He sneezes and feels his eyes spring back open as a pall of dirty orange smoke skews towards him on the morning breeze.

Flames, blood-red and jumping, on the other side of the main street. Less than fifteen metres from where he is standing, projecting himself out to the edge of the burning town.

Before he knows it, Lachlan's rushing barefooted across the bitumen, swearing at where the jags of blue metal stab his skin, to find a small grassfire in the spare block by the footpath. It's the same block where he saw the little boy sitting in Pippa's gutted RAV4 and now there's a Nyamal man in tradie's gear standing on the verge. He safeguards his eyes from the smoke with a flat hand, watching and mostly unbothered by the creep of flames trying to reach further towards the main road. He has his left hand planted on the shoulder of a boy – who he's guessing is the man's son – and Lachlan realises, through his panic, this is the same boy he saw sitting in Pip's wrecked car God-knows-how-long-ago. Feels like a lifetime ago that he shipwrecked in the Cliff.

The man sees Lachlan there, wide-eyed and with his mouth gaping, and smiles. 'Some'a the kids waitin' for the bus got bored and set the grass on fire. Little buggers.' He waves a hand, as if this might soothe Lachlan's pinched expression. 'I've called the firies. They'll be here soon.'

That should make him feel better but he lingers. Hangs beside the man and his son and the flames fill his eyes. Watches how they spread back towards the blue-leaved mallees in the dead creek, setting them ablaze now swift as a matchhead just struck. The fire stalks towards the bulk of town.

Peering up at the stone façade of the police station and the Neave house, Lachlan thinks, *Let it burn.*

Maybe the fire will cleanse the town's soul, all the death and loss it's built upon.

As if by magic, when Lachlan bids his farewell to the man and the boy, he turns to find the congress has already set up on the verandah, smiling at him with love and not at the worrying pall rising darkly at his back. 'A bit of excitement,' Glen chirps.

Lachlan can't help but beam stupidly back and be struck by an odd sense of gratefulness. That his little brother vanishing has delivered him to this place, the foothills by the river, and into the arms of these wonderful, mad bastards.

He wanders over and takes his camp chair and June frowns at him. 'What ya do that for?'

He laughs, lifts his hands in defence. 'Oi, wasn't me.'

They sit in their camp chairs and watch the fire truck pull up – fetched in a hurry by some locals from the Emergency Services shed on the edge of town. For a moment, hearing the heft of the motor, Lachlan wonders if it's the return of that Kenworth. The Dutchman drunk out of his mind. Not sure why this sends a shiver up his sweaty back.

The bored-looking young men unravel their hose from beside the truck as the Nyamal man and his son watch on, flick at the black ash which has settled on the fronts of their shirts.

'Spray us!' June bellows at them. 'We're cookin' over 'ere!'

'If we got hit with that thing, June, it'd knock us through the wall,' Pippa tells her with a chuckle.

Shrubb becomes tired of watching the firefighters put out the last of the grassfire and his eyes stray to Lachlan. 'Forgot to ask yesterday. How's that lovely girl ya got down in the big smoke? When ya gunna introduce us to her anyway?'

The smoke from the grassfire has cast an aureate colour across the face of the newborn sun, lending their shadows a bluish hue where they're stamped upon the concrete. 'Not sure there'll even be a phone call today,' Lachlan confesses, then coughs a bit with the smoke. 'Actually, I think she's losing patience with me a bit. Wants me back home already.' He thinks about this, clearing his burning throat. 'I would've thought she'd be more understanding, you know? About all ...' He struggles to sum it up in one word. '*This*.'

'She must have rocks in her head,' Shrubb says, but it brings no comfort. He looks at Lachlan a moment longer with dimming light in his eyes, same as Pippa now. 'Ya just need to rock up back down there and sweep her off her bloody feet, that's what ya gotta do.'

Pippa turns to raise her eyebrows at him. 'And you know something about that, do you Jim?' she asks, then includes June in her stare.

June laughs. 'I waited over a decade for treatment like that and I sure-as-hell never got it.'

Shrubb ignores this. 'Too right, I bloody do!' Sparked to life, he jumps to his feet, toes wriggling in his thongs. 'How's the first dance comin' along?'

Lachlan looks up at him. 'Eh?'

'The first dance? Ya know, after ya've taken ya vows, ya have the first dance. Ya said ya been engaged for six months. I hope ya been practisin.'

Lachlan smiles, shakes his head. 'Nup. Not really.'

'Ridiculous. Up ya get. Let's go.'

Lachlan twists towards Pippa. 'Don't look at me,' she tells him.

Shrubb takes him by both forearms now and draws him from the camp chair. In the otherworldly light cast through the smoke, Shrubb shows him where to put his hands and Lachlan awkwardly acquiesces. The fire truck grumbles back to life and leaves without one of the congress turning to watch. The father and son the other side of the road see it off instead. The father lifts his son up onto his shoulders so the boy can watch the truck disappear back down the Cliff's main street.

'Right, I'll lead,' Shrubb tells him. 'Coz ya never done this before.'

Lachlan doesn't want to offend Shrubb but still chuckles. 'I don't think I can do this.'

'S'fine. Follow me lead. Ya'll do fine.'

Glen's reclined in his seat, hands behind his head. 'This is just lovely.'

Each time Shrubb takes a step, Lachlan fears stepping on his foot, crushing his toes. Instead, he falls into Shrubb's rhythm, lurching into the space Shrubb's body just occupied. Senses himself ripped into the tailwind of something bigger than the two of them, something concealed in the choking smog still rolling off the empty block across the road. Into these weirdly elegant, gliding motions, and once they've picked up a nice sway, bodies joined despite the physical distance between them, June hoots with delight.

'See?' Shrubb cries. 'You're a bloody natural.'

Lachlan laughs back. 'Shit. I guess, I am.'

When he turns back to the others, they're all smiling uncontrollably, but he likes the way Pippa's looking at him most of all. He imagines this is how she used to look at his little brother. He imagines this is what love looks like.

'I had to show Elizabeth how to do this, see?' Shrubb announces, his voice as assured and steadfast as Lachlan's ever heard it. 'I learned meself just so I could teach her. We danced at her graduation like this, a lot like this. I remember that night thinkin' it was good practice for the day she'd eventually get married.'

Now the grassfire's died out, the smoke is clearing, though it's still lit Jasper Cliff's main street with a blood-orange glow, and the shadows of the two men perform their wedding dance upon the pub verandah.

That is until Shrubb's head hits Lachlan hard in the chest and he thinks he's fucked up, finally stepped on the man's foot and Shrubb's now clawing back at Lachlan in agony.

Then he senses how Shrubb jolts against him and for a moment he wonders if the man is in the thrall of a seizure, receiving a vision of some kind. Pitched across the distance between here and the foothills, a terrible gift slungshot across space all the way from the Rift.

It's not until he hears Shrubb's sobs that the dance dies, quick as the smoke blowing over. Feels his arms wrap around the grieving father to hold him. The others watching without a sound, Lachlan embracing Shrubb and telling him lies, telling him everything's going to be just fine.

In the Rift, the intruder wriggles in its chamber of fierce, superheated rock. Some days it might cook at inhuman temperatures, seething with enormous energy. Soaking it all up until it feels so much bigger than itself.

Listens to the ravine beyond. Still no visitors come. Though it's been trying to lure someone, anyone, for years. Strangers and bushwalkers and truck drivers. Over a hundred years, in the seeds of each generation grown and withered and fallen like spoilt fruit. It's tried to entice sons and fathers and the fathers of those fathers. Some have made it close but are readily deterred at the last moment, distracted by the muddle of their own lives.

It's lured the two brothers from the cold south, burying visions in their skulls since their first epileptic fits. It was easier to do with those gifted at birth with the Sight. Even the pale Englishwoman, ever since her Boeing clapped down over in Sydney. It's buried little secrets in the back of her mind, taunting and mostly ugly, trying to whisper her to the opening of the ravine.

Time has slopped and spluttered through the intruder's fingers so much faster than it did with the humans, and still it can remember its brethren. Herded by the Afghan cameleers out into the interior to point out the fastest, safest way through the strangest of these alien deserts. The intruders would group together at night away from the Muslim men by their fires, and soak in the shine of the moon.

The boredom set in after no time at all. After all, the Afghans only wanted them for one thing only, when the intruder and its siblings possessed so much more power. So they started burying little truths in the minds of the Muslim men as they slept. Secrets long buried, mostly skeletons in the family closet, in their dreams. Secrets but also, once the intruder and its siblings got bored enough, just plain lies. In the dark, under the pallor of the moon, they'd chuckle dryly as the Afghans began to suspect they were losing their minds.

They were cast out soon after, once the Muslim men had crossed the last of these immense deserts. One left behind deep in the Little Sandy Desert. One closer to the outskirts of Cue. The intruder had been the last, abandoned right here on the fringes of the Coongan River.

The intruder can only guess where its brethren might be now. If it might find them where they fled in the watery slush of time. Until then, until it has worked up the courage to go in search, it'd have to make do with whoever else might be close by.

Hell, the intruder would even make do with a wandering Shorthorn. Just so it could impart its glorious knowing, to someone, something. Anything.

They all wait, trying not to share anxious glances with each other, after Shrubb takes off.

Lachlan had been restless to return to the hills by the Coongan River but knows he can't now, can't leave the others as they keep their eyes firmly locked on the footpath. Waiting with hope at first, but as the hours have oozed by, he can sense the worry pouring off Pippa, June and Glen like BO exuding from their armpits on this stinker of a day.

When Shrubb still hasn't arrived by six o'clock, as Jasper Cliff sharpens its shadows and the galahs wail their loudest, Lachlan decides to go for a walk and search for him. He crosses the main street and there's still a tang of smoke in the air from the grassfire. He is surprised the police paddy wagon hasn't shown up again; Connor and Raeside returning to find the children responsible for setting the dry grass ablaze. Still chasing those misdemeanours they can control, instead of searching for those people there's no longer any hope of finding.

He winds his way down past the Shire Office and the deli, doesn't look at Elizabeth Shrubb or Ricky Muswell beseeching him with their sad paper eyes on the wall, and finally reaches what used to be the creek. From down here, he can see how far the little grassfire spread earlier, how it's stamped a huge blackspot in the spare block. And as Lachlan rustles through some blue-leaved mallees, he sees there's a figure lying outstretched in the centre of the burn mark.

Catching breath so hard his ribs ache at him, Lachlan suspects it's the little boy he saw earlier with his father, the one sitting in the ruin of Pippa's RAV4 on that first morning as if time would never touch him. Similarly arranged here, below the red welt of sky, untouchable, even as the world was burning all about him.

But then Lachlan spots those flappy thongs, still attached to feet where they jut in the air.

Shrubb.

He pitches into a full-on trot, despite the lacerating heat at dusk, heart swelling to think the idiot might've hurt himself. The mallees scratch at his side as he races through and almost sprains an ankle in the pebbles littering the creek bed. The hopeless fool lies in the huge burn spot but there's not a graze on him.

A fire inside Lachlan is quickly doused when he sees the Woodstock bottle in Shrubb's grip. Another empty cast to the side.

'Dickhead,' Lachlan blathers before he realises it. Thinks he should probably show some more sympathy. 'We had no idea where you were.'

Shrubb glares up at him with apologetic eyes. Lachlan sees now the scoured earth is still smoking ever so slightly, lifting in pale grey tendrils around them both. 'I'm so so sorry, Lach.' He lets his head thunk back into the blackened sand. 'Thought I was doin' the right thing, honest to God about that.'

'Don't worry about any of that now,' Lachlan tells him, trying to will some softness into his tone and failing woefully. 'Let's get you back to the others, hey?'

'I didn't lie. I need ya to know that. But it's eatin' me up inside.

And I got to thinkin', like not tellin' the truth is still kinda a lie. Got to thinkin' maybe holdin' back the truth is even worse than a lie. Knowin' ya could save someone a whole lotta pain and not lettin' 'em have that.' He swigs from the bottle. 'I'm a selfish fucken prick. Never been under any illusions about that.'

Finally, as Lachlan steps onto the darker, crunching ground, he hears all this. Lets it filter through. Goes rigid. 'What are you talking about?'

Not tellin' the truth is still kinda a lie.

Shrubb opens his mouth, the dry clag of tears sticky on his face, crawling with flies. Then cuts himself off, eyes flicking to someone in the unseen. For the briefest moment, Lachlan suspects it's that monstrous conglomerate shadow he sensed near the prospector's memorial, that clawing mass having returned for him.

'He's drunk,' June says.

Lachlan looks up, sees her watching from just a couple of metres away. Wonders how long she's been there, listening.

'Talkin' nonsense,' she adds, but now she sounds scared. 'Too much to drink. Again.'

Lachlan ignores her. He kneels beside Shrubb, touches his shoulder. 'What are you trying to tell me, Shrubb?'

'I was tryin' to protect Pip. S'why I never said nothin'. I love her so fucken much, she doesn't really have a clue how much. Couldn't let her get hurt.' He lets the Woodstock spill at his side, mostly all drunk now anyway, so it's not much of a loss. 'Then you showed up. And ya were a lot like Toby, and I couldn't let ya get hurt the same way.'

Fire seethes in Lachlan's eyes as if he might reignite the untouched grass which remains, and he seizes Shrubb by the neck of the shirt. 'What are you saying?!' he cries. 'Did you hurt Toby?!'

Looks up, June closer now. Unmoved by his rage. 'That's not what he's sayin',' she tells him.

He directs his next question up at her. 'Do you two know what happened to him?'

She shakes her head.

'But I know where ya can find out what happened,' Shrubb admits finally, and Lachlan's hands release their grip on his shirt.

'Don't,' June just manages to get in.

But Shrubb says it anyway, 'I know where the Rift is.'

9

'First time I found it, I'd just turned twenty-one,' Shrubb says, words slurring a little. 'S'was the day after me birthday, actually. Always been a bit of a loner, I guess. Mum and Dad wanted to throw me this big shindig, but to tell the truth, all I wanted was to be on me own. Wander around in the spinifex. How I spent most'a me time anyway.'

When he smiles now, all Lachlan wants to do is throttle the fucker. Only an hour earlier, he would've found that smile endearing. Even a comfort.

'Granddad was the first one to tell me about the Rift. He'd never seen it himself but he worked with this Pole who reckons he stumbled across it back in the day. Gave a pretty decent description of it too. He even did a sketch of the thing. I've got it back at the house somewhere. Put it in a frame.'

Now they're all gathered around him outside the pub again, the grog smell is so strong Lachlan feels his mouth water. A drink would be good right about now.

'I was never actively lookin' for the thing. And I think that's how it gets ya sometimes. *It* chooses when it wants to be found. *You* don't have much choice in the matter really. Ya could have all the money and equipment in the world, GPS and satellites and the whole shebang, but if the Rift don't wanna be found, it won't be.'

'Get on with it,' Lachlan tells him.

June shoots him a fierce expression. 'Ya wanted to hear his story, ya let him tell it the way he wants to.'

Shrubb's too drunk to worry about this interruption anyway. Takes a moment to meet Pippa's eyes, until she squeezes his hand. Only then does he go on, 'Yeah, so anyway, the day after me birthday, and it was real close to dark and I stumble up to this really thin gorge. More like a ravine, I guess. Or a gully maybe. Not sure what the difference is really. Bit of water at the openin' of it. Coupla euros there drinkin' and they took off when they saw me. It wouldn't have grabbed my attention otherwise. Just looked like anywhere else in those hills. I probly woulda just walked on past it if it wasn't for that little bit'a water.'

'How can ya be sure it was the real thing?' Glen asks now, leaning closer like a little kid savouring every word of a ghost story.

'Well, I wasn't. Not at first. Stumbled down there and saw the cliff face with the big crack in it. Didn't even occur to me at the time that it looked a lot like that sketch my grandfather gave me when I was a tyke.' He takes a breath, holding Pippa's eyes still. 'It was only when I went up to the cliff face, went up and touched the rock. Then I knew it was the Rift.'

Pippa's voice shudders, 'How?'

'I saw somethin', but in my head. Like a movie playin' inside me skull.' Now Shrubb starts to tremble, shivering like he's on the tundra, even as the sweat streams off him. 'Saw me uncle actually. Was always close to me uncle. Was always good to me.

He'd take me out bush-bashing some weekends and we'd tent it overnight. As far away as Carawine, and Dooleena Gorge. Had this camp oven in which he'd knock up the nicest bloody apricot chicken you can imagine.' Shrubb shakes his head to recount this, suck at some cola spit in the corner of his mouth. 'He was good to me, kind. Loved me. I really didn't think there was a better human being than me uncle. But the Rift showed me somethin' very different.'

Now Shrubb swallows hard and for a moment Lachlan wonders if he'll go on. 'I guess, I thought I had an idea of who me uncle was. But the Rift, man …' He shakes his head. 'It shows you the truth. No bullshit. It shows ya how it really is.'

'What do you mean?' Lachlan snaps, the impatience clearer, colder in his voice now.

'It showed me what my uncle done to some young blokes,' he explains, voice shuddering. 'Most'a them looked like they were just fucken teenagers. Barely outta school. Christ.' Shrubb rests his forehead in his hands, as if he can see it so clearly all these years later. 'Musta been when he was livin' back down in Perth. He'd get them on the piss at the pub and then take them back to his van. Looked like the seventies to me, with how they dressed and that. Flares, they're called, aren't they? Everyone smokin' joints. Then after he took what he wanted from 'em in the back of van, he'd push 'em out the door and just drive off, listenin' to the Bee Gees on the radio like it wasn't a thing at all.'

Pippa's hardly aware of it, but her sweaty fingers have curled into Shrubb's even harder. He looks up at her, teary again. 'Wasn't a big drinker before that, Pip. I really wasn't.'

'Only got bad from then on,' June confirms from just out of

sight, looking more slumped and defeated than Shrubb now.

'Kept wire brushes in that van. Other things from around the house. He used them on those young blokes who were too tanked to defend themselves.' Shakes his head, lips wet with panicked slobber. 'After it finished showin' me all that horrible shit, I ran. I shit you not, man,' he says, still addressing Lachlan. 'I ran all the way home.'

'We don't blame ya, Shrubby,' Glen mutters.

'Swore I'd never go back anywhere near the Rift again. No way in hell.' Shaking his head so violently from side to side that his next admission arrives with his face obscured. 'And then Liz disappeared.'

Pippa squeezes his hand harder, turns from him to June. 'You thought it might show you what happened to her. Where she was.'

'We were callin' the coppers every day,' June says. 'And I mean, literally every day. Pleadin' for information. Both of us sleepin' in the car outside the station in the Bar. Every day for a year and a half after she went missin'. Until they told us we couldn't do that anymore. No one could tell us a thing. It was like she vanished into thin air as far as they were concerned. No leads, no suspects, no evidence. No nothin'.'

'That whole time, I was thinkin' about it,' Shrubb admits, shaking on the spot. Now Glen stands, biting his lips, and rests a hand on Shrubb's shoulder. 'What it'd showed me about me uncle, nothin' human could possibly know that. It had to be somethin' else, ya know? I dunno, like a god maybe or somethin' like that. Somethin' that saw the world different to us. Saw more of the world than we ever could hope to. So maybe it knew what had happened to our baby girl too?'

'And I didn't try talk him out of it either,' June admits. 'I just wanted my Elizabeth back home. Safe.' She looks over at Shrubb. 'With us.'

'I can't believe you didn't tell me,' Lachlan hears himself growl. He fires from his chair, hangs above Shrubb with menace. 'You need to tell me where it is right now. You shouldn't have kept this from me.' Then glances at Pippa. 'From *us*.'

'But this is the thing I'm tryin' to tell ya,' he whimpers. 'It doesn't always show ya what ya want to see. It didn't show me what happened to Liz. It showed me …' Now he falters, 'Other things. All stuff from the goldrush days. Things so fucken awful no one should ever see. Or even bloody know about. Stuff the coppers did to blackfellas. Stuff the prospectors did to each other. A fucken horror show ya wouldn't believe.'

'And I'm guessing that's the last time you went back?' Lachlan spits. 'Coz you got scared.' Swallows hard but forces the next accusation out clear as day, 'Coz you're a coward.'

'Enough,' Glen snaps at him, no real warning in it.

'If it was my daughter, I would've been there every day. I would've stood there and took it all, seen it all, just to know what happened to her. Not lost my nerve and spent the past ten years destroying my brain with that shit.' He jabs a finger at the Woodstock bottle at their feet. 'Just so I didn't have to think about it anymore.'

A shadow now cast on Shrubb's face, Lachlan finds himself wanting to reel back his outburst.

'You say that now,' says Shrubb. 'But ya haven't seen what it wants to show ya yet. Don't be surprised if ya find yaself in this very same position,' Shrubb tells him, looking down over himself. 'And in no fucken time at all.'

Pippa tries to ignore Lachlan, touches Shrubb's wrist so he twists back to her. '*I* need to know,' she says softly. 'I understand you were trying to protect me. And I love you for that, Jim. But I need to know where Toby is. I don't care what price I have to pay.'

His jaw firms up, locking into place. 'It won't show ya what ya want to see, Pip. In fact, it might just break you.'

'Still. Whatever it is,' she says, and joins Lachlan in standing. 'I need to see it.'

Glen brings his ute around, parks it the other side of the bowsers. Once he steps from the driver's seat, he jounces his keys up in the air, a muted darkness in his eyes now. He sees June unable to watch any of this from the verandah, too furious with them to bother staring daggers anymore.

Pippa steps up to him. 'Thanks for doing that.'

Glen turns back to her, squinting. 'You really believe all this stuff, Pip?' Looks around, chewing uncertainly on his dry bottom lip. 'Sounds like a whole lotta mumbo-jumbo to me, mate. I like a good story round the campfire as much as the next man. But this stuff?'

The question catches her out, leaves her wondering. 'I'm not sure. I guess, I've never really had to think about it before. Not seriously anyway. Not until I met Toby. But he believed in it. Hard not to after he experienced what he said he experienced.'

'It coulda just been one of his fits though, right?' Glen says, letting his hand droop, the one with the keys in his fist. 'All in his head maybe?' He nods back towards the verandah. 'Same with

Shrubb. After the abuse he's put his body and mind through all these years.'

Pippa acknowledges that, nods. 'Maybe, yeah.' She turns to watch Lachlan hold open the back door for Shrubb, letting him collapse into the back seat blearily. 'But what if it isn't? What if this thing is real and it can show us where Toby is?' She shrugs. 'That's not a risk I'm willing to take. This thing being able to help, and us not doing a thing about it. That's not something I can just ignore.'

With that, he glances at June one last time. Then gently takes Pippa's hand, nestles the car keys into her palm. 'Be careful. I'll hold down the fort. Keep an eye on old girl here.'

'Please do.' Pippa smiles, then catches Glen out with a peck on the cheek. Thinks she even sees him blush a little.

She goes across the front of the dual cab, opens the driver's side door. Only now dares to look back up at June and meet her fierce eyes.

'This isn't right, Pip,' she calls after them, a bleak croak in her voice. 'Makin' him revisit all this. He's been through enough as it is. Ya should know that.'

'I'll look after him,' Pippa tells her. 'I promise.'

Shutting the door behind her, all she wants to do is headbutt the steering wheel, for what she's doing, for what she's already done. Looks across at Lachlan, determined as ever, and already facing the road impatiently. The smell of alcohol overwhelming in here, and she wonders how much Shrubb has drunk already, but when she twists in her seat to look, she finds him with a hip flask of whiskey, sipping.

Pippa looks back at Lachlan. 'He needs courage,' Lachlan tells her, resolute, as if this is any explanation at all.

She cranks the engine, already regretting this. 'Means to an end, huh?'

Shrubb directs them to a rough sand track which wends away from the side of the creek behind the Neave house, and soon they're awash with blue-leaved mallees and hummock grassland. Can see where the kids from town bring their trailbikes through here, cutting different zigzags out into the spinifex.

Shrubb takes an extra-long slug from the hip flask, then clears his throat. 'Here. Pull over here. By that rock.'

A lonely chunk of basalt by the side of the road, and once Pippa's beside it, she puts Glen's ute into park and looks back at Shrubb. Never seen anyone shaking so violently, like a lone sprig rocking around in the wind.

'That way.' Shrubb points towards the foothills. 'Two, maybe three ks.'

'You're coming with us,' Lachlan says, without looking into the back seat.

Shrubb's quiet a spell, then says, 'I swore I'd never go back to that place. Not after what it showed me last time. Do whatever ya want to me, but I can promise ya this, I'm not movin' from this fucken seat.'

'You're showing us the way.'

'I swore on my daughter's life never to go back near that thing, Lachie,' Shrubb explains darkly. 'Good luck gettin' me to break that promise.'

Lachlan makes her jump behind the steering wheel when he bawls, 'Get outta the car!'

Pippa grits her teeth at Lachlan. 'Stop!'

'I'd rather bash me own brains out on that rock than go back there,' he tells Pippa directly now. Finally, his jaw has quit chattering, and she can see that he means it now this uneasy stillness has fallen over him.

'You don't have to come,' she says, fending off the urge to reach over and confiscate the hip flask in his hand. 'Just wait for us here, okay?'

He nods.

'I'll leave the engine running so you've got the aircon. That way, you won't cook.'

Lachlan looks at her furiously. 'How can we be sure if he's not going to take off and leave us here?'

'Just get out of the fucking car.'

Means to an end, she reminds herself.

Pippa reaches into the back seat to grip Shrubb's hand now but can't look at the opaque numbness in his eyes for long. And to know she's played some part in this. Lachlan mostly, but her too. She tries to imagine what that would be like, seeing her own uncle – a man she loved so dearly she learned to sign so she could talk to him after he went deaf – doing those things to drunk men in the back of a panel van. Dark desires undisclosed; only the Rift had known, had seen. Pippa thinks she might've lost her mind after seeing something like that. Could have turned to drink.

'We'll be back,' Pippa tells him, but realises she's staring down at the hip flask.

'It might not be about Tobes,' he whimpers. 'Just be prepared for that. It sees everythin' that happens here. Back to the goldrush. It saw everythin.' Another slug, another failed attempt at courage. 'And it'll show you too.'

She had a dream last night. Funny, dreams. How they sluice away like dirty water between her fingers when she tries to get a hold on them after waking – in her bed without Toby still.

Looking at Lachlan's marching back, clattering his way through the scratchy spinifex, she thinks what a sour substitute she's been landed with. How disappointing. 'He could be lying,' Lachlan says back over his shoulder.

'Why would he do that?'

'Like he said, he wanted to protect you.'

'I don't think he has any reason to lie. Not now.'

Smirks. 'He's been lying to us from the start.'

Her irate voice so loud it echoes, 'Just shut up and walk.'

Last night's dream is slowly returning to her as she moves. It was about Glen. Weird, she's never dreamed about Glen before. At least not that she can remember. She dreamed she was trapped in some dark, dank chamber. The only light visible through two tiny peepholes. Through these she could see Glen's face and he was stumbling around like he'd been drinking, though his skin was speckled with blood. It was only once she'd touched these peepholes, had gone to call out to him and wake him from his stumbling stupor, she found these were holes opened in flesh. They looked like they'd been made by snake fangs.

Pippa almost walks straight into Lachlan when he suddenly stops and hesitates, then halts to stare at him. 'Who needs courage now?' she digs.

He doesn't answer, just points at a black puddle at the mouth of a thin ravine. A dead calf beside it, skin barely hanging onto its bones like a wet jumper.

'I think we're here.'

Pippa picks around the edge of the fetid-smelling water but now he's here, rooted to the dirt, Lachlan finds he can't move any further. Only half of him ever believed this, since Pippa told him about the Rift, and Toby's search for it. Things like the Rift exist in his brother's short stories – the realm of imagination – not in the real world.

But if that's true, why can't he take another step?

Pippa glances back at him, fresh disdain painted on her face. 'What are you doing?'

'I'm not sure …' is all he can get out, lips going blubbery. The disquiet roots him to the spot. How Shrubb says it shows you things, Toby too. How it sees into the past, knows what most have forgotten, or wilfully wiped from their memories.

He recalls all those names on the memorial. Each morbid description of fate's skeletal hand met.

Died 1896. Stabbed to death by his brother.

Died 1900. Speared through the face by Nyamal warriors, payback for a rape.

Died 1899. Gored to death by a neighbour's bull.

'I'm not sure I want to see those things,' Lachlan finally admits.

He feels a hand meet his, soft fingers interlocked, and sees it's Pippa's – not the terrible hand of fate awaiting. He looks into her smiling eyes. Where only moments ago, she was pissed with him, he sees she can put all that aside. Finally, he's found his courage.

'I'll be right here,' she tells him. 'I'm with you all the way.'

She only releases Lachlan's hand once they've edged around the sickly puddle, both holding their noses because of the stink of the putrefied water.

She doesn't intend to let go, but she thinks she might let go of herself. Enclosed by the red walls of the ravine, she's not sure she's ever seen anything so beautiful. As if her entire life, she's been flat on her back on a gurney, and only now, since taking this first step towards the cliff face at the end of the ravine, someone has hit her in the chest with a defibrillator.

The Rift looks much as Shrubb described it – a tall crimson face of rock with a thin rupture through its middle, winged on both sides by glossy heaps of wirewood. Pippa feels the rocky floor sliding away under her. It's as if they've stepped into some liminal enclave. Their pasts and futures malleable as putty in the palm of some coarse, scaly hand yet to be divulged.

When she steps over to the riven cliff face, it hums a glorious blood-red. Night imminent as the sun fiercens over the top of the ravine wall. As she reaches to touch the Rift's skin, she half expects it to be velveteen by how smooth it looks.

'Stop,' Lachlan says.

Shocked out of her trance, she turns to him. But can't find the words.

'We don't have to do this,' he says.

She would've liked to be here with Toby. High like this, immured by ageless basalt walls. Just the idea of it is so romantic her belly rollercoasters. She hasn't let herself feel it, not fully, until now. She'd do anything to have him back by her side, his fingers interlocked with hers.

'This is wrong,' Lachlan goes on. 'We don't know what this thing is.' He nods at the Rift. 'And maybe we're not meant to.' He peers into the darkened crack in the chert and she joins him and notices how bare it is. Usually a plant or young tree might grow from a rift in rock like this. And it's far too burnished, as if fashioned from clay. 'It might not show us anything to do with Toby, but it'll show us something. And look at what that something has done to Shrubb.'

'But we're here now,' Pippa mutters. Mere inches from the cliff face.

'We can find him,' Lachlan takes a step towards her. 'I only just realised that, now everything's falling apart. Took it falling apart for me to see.'

See? But what am I about to see? she wonders. *What's it about to show me?*

She peers into the patient dark of the Rift. 'You're just scared,' she tries to throw at him, but it falls limp in the baking air.

'We can find Toby. You and me. Together.' That last word stops her, makes her look back. 'And not just you and me. Shrubb too. June. Glen. All of us.' Now he doesn't even look at the Rift. 'We don't need this thing, Pip.'

But maybe I want *to see?*

'And once we find Toby, and we will find him, we can look for the others. Elizabeth. Aunty Belle's daughter. All those faces on the wall. We can find them all. We just have to do it together.'

She swallows, knows he's right. Finally, more like Toby than she ever thought possible. Able to see to the truth of things. All she wants to do is throw herself into his arms.

But she looks back, one last time, at the Rift. Behind the warm cheek of chert, something moves. She sees it through the thin crack in the rock, then hears a raspy unfurling.

'There's something in there,' Pippa says dreamily. 'Some kind of animal.'

The intruder, she thinks.

'Come on. Fuck this thing. Whatever it is,' Lachlan says, reaching to take her hand again. 'Let's go find him.'

Now an eye through the splinter, the iris shutters in and out, and it sees her. Sees her and beyond her, across the lazy eddies of time and blood-fat tick of land beside the Coongan River. Sees only because of the requisite tetrachromats in that all-seeing eye – able to see to the core of things.

Lachlan reaches to rest a hand on her shoulder but then leaps away and flounders in the wirewood to escape, shrieking. Pippa looks down at the scaly hand extending from the Rift. Four fingers and thumb, but it can't be human, not olive-green like this, armoured and reptilian.

It gently wraps its fingers around Pippa's wrist. The feel of it against her skin is rough but also, somehow, like the touch of someone trusted, benevolent, a seer imparting some great knowing.

She sees Lachlan over there in the wirewood, scrambling and panting, his eyes white as milk. And his brother.

Toby fords his ute down a rough track under a loom of river red gums. A slew of dirty water below and there's too much of a current for it to be the Coongan River. Once he parks, he sits staring at the water for a while.

He's wearing the same clothes he was wearing that last night he spent with her.

The drive has cleared his head now, especially with the sun blazing down on his shoulders. Toby steps from the ute, finds his way down to the bank. He shouldn't have screamed at her. He loves Pippa more than he ever thought he could love someone. Still didn't mean he could be a father for her. It wasn't ever anything he could do for someone else.

Toby kneels above the coursing water, the surface too maroon and muddy to throw back his reflection. But the galahs shriek and shit white stripes into the creek and he's brought back to the joy of this place. Him and this. It's what he's always wanted. Him and this, but he's shocked now to find he wants something else just as much.

He wants him and this, but he also wants her.

A pinched smile on his face. Then Toby laughs. 'Yeah, okay,' he tells the urgent creek. 'That sounds pretty good.'

He peers back at his parked car, a completely new colour after the mud roads he's gunned along to clear all the junk from his mind. It's only an hour and a half back to Jasper Cliff. An hour and a half back to Pippa.

But when he goes to stand, twists on the spot to make back for the car, his foot catches on the rim of a tyre half buried in the sand. Dumped off the back of a truck by someone passing through and souring here for twenty years and now it throws Toby off balance and sends him headfirst into the running creek. Punching through the water, he feels his temple clump against a snag of red gum all slimy just below the surface.

He sees his own blood in the toilet bowl water. And he's not conscious for much longer, only vaguely aware of the current wrapping around him and lugging him off in the opposite direction to where the rain has been falling since midnight.

Not conscious for much longer, though Toby's just aware of this surprising warmth spreading through his body. Shapes of river red gums above him, a congress of tall trees watching him go. So much love, taking him somewhere else.

The vision only stops when the lizard hand unclenches her wrist. She looks down groggily to watch it slowly withdraw into the crack in the cliff face, snaked back into the Rift by whatever arm that hand was attached to deeper within.

Once it's gone, Lachlan stumbles out of the wirewood. He grabs her by the arm, the same one the lizard hand gripped her by, and drags her clear of the Rift. 'Holy shit,' he bellows. 'Are you okay? Your bloody eyes rolled back in your head like you were having a fit.' He edges away from the cliff, cautious not to get too close in case the hand shoots back out of the crack. 'What did you see?' he asks, almost like he no longer wants to know. 'Did it show you something?'

Standing here, only a metre or so from the Rift, Lachlan right in front of her, and yet most of her is still back with Toby, above the burble of the creek, the smell of fresh water.

'He's gone,' she tells him. 'But he wasn't in any pain. He wasn't scared.' Now she clutches his hand in hers, can still feel that rough patch of skin where the intruder grabbed her.

'He's just gone.'

Lachlan asks her one question after another along the drive back to town, unnerved by her sudden ease. He pulls up beside the bowsers and she peers out at Glen and June still standing there.

Looks like they haven't moved an inch since she left. It seems like a decade's been and gone, while they've probably only been out at the Rift for an hour or so.

Pippa steps out of the car, watching Lachlan join her. She can see he's about to ask another question – frazzled by his need to understand – when there's a loud crash beside the ute. The hip flask Lachlan bought from the deli: Shrubb's just pitched it out the window. It lies there, unharmed. Shrubb hasn't moved from the back seat since they left; it's hot even with the aircon, the sweat darkening his shirt down to his abdomen.

Pippa looks back into the cab. 'Jim?'

'Get Glen for me.' Won't look at her. Drunker than she's ever seen him.

Pippa turns to Glen and he hurries over, June following with rue in her eyes for Lachlan. 'What's goin' on, my old mate?' Glen asks gently.

'Can ya take me to me brother's? Over in the Bar.' His head rocks around on his shoulders like his neck's made of rubber. 'He'll get me sober. He knows what to do. He'll kick me arse if I reach for anothery.' Then he seems to firm up, hold Glen's stare. 'Please, Glen?'

'You got it,' Glen answers straight away. Then turns to Pippa with sympathy in his eyes, determined, and holds his hand out for the keys.

Pippa goes to say something but then looks at Shrubb again, his uncaring expression. She lets the keys fall.

'You're going to come back though, right Jim?' Pippa asks through the open window, throat scratched and straining.

He won't answer, still won't even look at her. June appears the other side of the ute, wrenches open the door and hugs the air out of Shrubb. Pippa thinks she hears one of them start to weep but she's not sure who. Whispers from the old lovers. Pippa hangs back with Lachlan.

June is the first to pull away. 'You call me tomorrow, okay?' she demands of him. 'First thing in the mornin'. No bloody excuses.'

'You got it, my love.'

Glen humphs in behind the steering wheel, looks back at Pippa and Lachlan. 'Be back in a few hours.' Then he grins at Lachlan, though there's some solemnity in it now. 'And you. Don't use all the bloody cold water.'

'Drive safe, please,' Pippa adds but it sounds hollow.

Those remaining outside the pub watch Glen's Triton cruise down the main street, passing the ghost gum now vacated by Aunty Belle. Pippa can see the back of Shrubb's head, black curls reaching out from under his sweaty cap, but he doesn't look back at her, or June.

He'll be reported missing by the end of the week but no one will ever find him, or the pieces of him. His face reshaped upon one of those missing persons posters at the deli. His face alongside that of his daughter's, watching the very few who happen to pass by as if they were the spectres and not him, now one of many quivering in that gallery of the lost.

10

Waiting, still always this waiting.

Waiting for Glen to return, they sit at the bar with no liquor and Lachlan listens to Pippa recount as best she can what she saw in her mind when the scaled hand emerged from the Rift and grabbed her. About halfway through, she breaks down in tears. Not so much tears of grief but solace. To know he'd gone the way he did is almost a blessing.

Lachlan listens, mostly perplexed. Can't understand why he's not crying. His little brother is dead, has been for over a month already. And in an accident – drowned in the roving current of some random creek, one among countless branching this or that side of Jasper Cliff. Guesses he's just numb, is all. Guesses, he too, was expecting something much, much worse.

He finds himself more concerned with comforting Pippa and they embrace, sweaty bodies pressed against each other. She has the physical presence of a giant grasshopper with her lankiness, her long neck. Her tears slowly subside and when they part again, he stares at the shiny bar top which hasn't felt the bottom of a whiskey glass in who-knows-how-long; strangely, Lachlan feels more lost now than when he didn't know what had happened to his little brother.

'His car will still be out there,' he mutters, just to say something. 'Maybe we should give Connor and Raeside a call? Give them an idea of where to look.'

Pippa nods, cleaning her face with a scrunched tissue. 'The only problem is we'd have to explain how we knew his car was out there. Or how we even have an idea of where it might be.'

Lachlan nods, slowly cottoning on. 'And if we tell them about what just happened, what the both of us just saw, they'll think we're mental. Or worse.' He considers this. 'They might think we were lying all along.'

The door to the pub's been left open and now Lachlan looks out there, he can see the hip flask Shrubb threw from the Triton earlier. Lazes there in the hot verandah glow. Lost, so fucken lost. Jasper Cliff flexes its corrugated-iron skin below the nine o'clock heat, humming with insects and the sleepy chirps of galahs in the ghost gums. The night's glorious soliloquy.

'Speaking of which,' Lachlan says. 'What the hell do I tell Mum? If I tell her that story, she'll call in the whitecoats.'

'I'm sure that's not true.' Pippa squeezes his wrist. 'You can only tell her what you saw. What I saw. I guess, she'll make up her own mind from there.'

When Lachlan finds her weepy eyes again, he experiences a flare of panic like a match struck inside his chest. 'And he wasn't in any pain? You're absolutely sure of that?'

Peaceful as it must've been, as she's described it, it was much less so on the outside. Watching her from the wirewood, Lachlan saw the lizard hand grip her and then she started to quake, body shuddering, eyes white as a full moon and rolling back as if the inside of her skull needed inspecting. Her fit by the Rift lasted only thirty seconds, but it was memorable to witness. Lachlan finally realises how frightful he must look to others in the throes of one of his seizures.

'I didn't just see him, like a movie in my head,' Pippa explains, 'But I could feel him. Could feel what he felt and thought. And he was coming back to me.' Her face breaks into a smile. 'You were right about him and how he felt about kids. Fatherhood was not something to be taken lightly. And I still don't think he'd changed his mind. But he also realised it didn't matter because he wanted to be here. With us. With me.'

Now Lachlan smiles back. 'I'm glad.'

'When he hit the water, he didn't even really feel the bump to his head. From what I felt, he wasn't conscious too much longer, couldn't even feel the cold rushing into his lungs. He looked up and could see the trees through the surface and there was this overwhelming sense of…' For a moment, she struggles to articulate what his little brother had felt in those last moments. 'Returning to something he'd left long ago.' Pippa examines the bar top thoughtfully, the globe of reflected light as if it held the Rift's memory. 'Something like that anyway.'

Still no tears, bereft but without the release. Possibly his burden to lug onwards into whatever waits for him next. Doesn't matter anyway, he thinks. He takes Pippa's hand and stands from his stool. He must care for Pippa right now – this precious woman his little brother loved. No time to think about how he might be feeling about all this. He'd choose numbness right now anyway.

'You need sleep,' he tells her, wrapping his spare hand around her back. 'Looks like you're about to fall off that stool.'

She glances at the open door. 'I wanted to wait for Glen to get back. Make sure he made it home okay.'

'I can do that. I want you to get some rest. What happened today was …'

Why even try form it into words? he wonders.

'Too much. Come on.'

She relents more easily than he expected, half-topples from the bar stool. They find the open doorway into her bedroom and the bed catches Lachlan's eye for a moment. That space Toby used to fill, empty, until Pippa launches herself, with a last-ditch-effort of strength, and thumps on the mattress.

Her breath already has some regularity about it so he turns to go but she must still be awake because she says, 'Lachie?' He turns back. Her face in the pillow so he can't see it. 'I'm glad you're here,' she tells him, partly muffled.

'Me too,' he says, grabbing the door handle to close it. 'And I'm not going anywhere either.'

Back in the bar, the open pub door beckons. He drifts his way out onto the empty verandah – he did that, emptied it. Destroyed Shrubb and June's trust, broke up their loving little family. But at least he has an answer, unfulfilling as it feels in this moment. The glint of light off the hip flask and when Lachlan picks it up, there's still a slosh of whiskey inside.

Lachlan unscrews the lid and drinks. Drinks a second time. Must be at least three shots' worth in here. He finishes the flask with a gargle, waits for the chemical warm and ease to kick in.

He returns to the bar. If there were bottles along the shelf, he'd refill the flask and keep drinking. Maybe he'd prove to be a solid stand-in now Shrubb's lost to the night too. As he's looking up at the shelves, he frowns to see that someone has graffitied the wooden beam above where the bottles of spirits should wait. Someone's carved a series of words up there.

He used to make fun of Toby when they were kids for how much he liked poetry; after all, it was a girl's thing to like poems, wasn't it? But Toby used to go on about it so much that he knows exactly who carved these words into the wooden beam before he left Jasper Cliff for the final time.

One need not be a chamber, it reads, *to be haunted.*

Then the sound of the Triton pulling up outside the bowsers, the chug of the motor louder than the quiet night beyond. Lachlan goes to look, half expecting to see Shrubb still in the back seat, mercifully having changed his mind and returned home.

But only Glen steps from the driver's side door. The back seat is empty.

He wakes from sleep thankfully vacant of dreams or wondering about his little brother's last moments on this earth. It requires tremendous effort to unstick himself from the bed until Lachlan remembers he'd been drinking yesterday. Whiskey always knocks him a bit off-kilter the morning after.

He straggles down to Pippa's room and knocks softly just below the handle. 'Pip?' he whispers.

She mustn't have woken in the night because the door is still unlocked. He turns the handle and lets it creak open a little to show the bed. But there's no Pippa. Assuming she's already woken and is out on the verandah, Lachlan is about to go and look when something catches his eye. The pillow. A sheet of folded paper on the pillow. For a moment he wonders if it's the missing persons poster showing Elizabeth Shrubb's smiling face that's somehow found its way in here, then shakes it off.

His heart sinks to find it's a letter. Unfolds it and reads Pippa's scratchy handwriting with the metallic tang of dread in his mouth.

Lachie,

I'm gone but not gone for good. I need you to understand that. And I don't want you to feel obligated towards the pub in any way. Just close the doors until I'm back. No one will really notice much anyway. It's not like we've been a hive of activity for a long time now.

I suppose the only thing I will ask is for you to watch out for June and Glen. Especially after everything that's happened. And Jim too, when he gets back from Marble Bar. I think some stubborn part of me has been distanced this whole time, rejecting their love, and it took seeing what I saw at the Rift to realise that annoying old idiom they print on Hallmark cards might be right after all: life is too short. It's far too short to be as pig-headed as I've been for any longer.

I need to be on my own for a bit. On the road for a while. But I won't be away from Jasper Cliff forever. Don't think I could be even if I tried. And when I'm back, I hope you'll be there too. I hope you stay. Not because it's what Toby would've wanted. Because it's what I want.

Love Pippa xx

He folds the sheet of paper and slides it lovingly into his pocket. Not entirely sure how he should feel about this, after all, he only found out his little brother was dead yesterday. He guesses there's no instructional manual for this crazy shit.

Out on the verandah, he finds he must've slept in. The layout of town is etched with blanched light, nearly midday. A fresh hollow in him to know Pippa's gone along with the others. Every day for the past week, since Connor and Raeside's visit, the one thing that's kept him going is the certainty that the congress would be waiting for him out on the warm concrete every morning, talking shit or arguing about this or that. Their lovely proximity had so quickly stapled him into place, stopping him from drifting off like so many others.

But then he turns to see Glen sitting in his camp chair already. 'What's goin' on?' he asks like nothing is different, though it's only the two of them on the hot concrete now. 'Where's Pip?'

Lachlan swallows hard to hear him ask this. 'Um. She needs some time out, I think. Some time to herself.'

Glen's eyes darken but then he slowly nods, as if this is perfectly understandable. 'Oh well, just me and you then, old son?'

Lachlan smiles. It won't be the same without the others, but at least this is something. 'Looks like it.'

They watch a Kenworth cruise into town, something about it strangely familiar. It pulls up at the bowsers and Lachlan sees the Dutchman behind the big wheel, the same who'd showed up here late in the night not so long ago, tanked out of his mind. The driver looks almost sheepish when he steps from the tall step and thumps onto the ground. Looks at Glen, then Lachlan. Eyes grim with another hangover.

Lachlan and Glen glance at each other. 'Ever run a pub and service station before?' Glen asks him, raising his eyebrows.

Lachlan shrugs. 'Well, I guess it's more service station than anything else. If that.'

He stares at the truck driver again. Makes a split-second decision. He walks over and fills the truck's tank with diesel. 'You look familiar,' the Dutch driver says tiredly, then winks.

Lachlan points at him, pretends to search his memory. 'Sorry, I didn't catch that,' he says, pointing at an ear. 'I don't fucking speak Australian.'

The truck driver laughs. 'That's the one.'

The nozzle clunks once the Kenworth's full and before Lachlan can think to ask for help, he hears Glen inside ringing up the till and shooting the shit cheerily with the Dutchman. He supposes he's running a small business now, for the time being anyway. He peers down the main street, as if he might glance up at the right moment to watch Pippa returning. But the forlorn town lounges immobile in sketchy outlines behind the mirage. Pippa long gone, like Shrubb, like Toby.

He saunters over to the verandah to find his camp chair, to sit and wait.

Rain. Bizarre to see it so soon. As if only Jasper Cliff cooks under a relentless sun, and the remainder of the world cools, frigid and grey.

It hazes the windscreen of Mrs Saelim's Datsun as Pippa rattles down the gravel road, the steering wheel shuddering in her hands. Should've known better than to risk this arse-end track to the

Auski Roadhouse, but she guesses she's craving a little adventure.

Only an hour and a half out of the Cliff, the sprinkling starts. Passing by a gold mine, Pippa watches a red plume boil up into the barbed wire sky from a carefully executed explosion. She parks at a spot nearby, under a parade of sheoaks where she and Toby had come for a picnic, then made love on the picnic blanket in the laving whir of the trees. She sits there in the same spot they had kissed and moved gently against each other, and she might've cried but she'd spent herself last night before going to bed.

Back in the crummy Datsun, and she holds her breath cruising along at a paltry 50 k's an hour, praying the little car has enough guts to get her to the Great Northern Highway. The Hamersley Range unfolds to her left and finally she bundles off the red road at the Auski Roadhouse lounging crappily one side of the long blacktop. She weaves between mammoth mining trucks, parks in a claggy puddle. Watches a girl walk past in a Rio Tinto jacket but rocking a G-banger through her wet and see-through shorts.

Pippa smiles, shakes her head. *We're not in the Cliff anymore.*

Out of the Datsun, the mizzle is delicate as spindrift against her face, and everything's turned to crimson mud; it all slurps and slathers as she rushes into the servo. Would've kept heading south once she got to the highway but her stomach has started to ache with hunger, so she orders some roadhouse grub – there's no grilled cheese and prawn nigiri on the menu.

Pippa sits at a bench by the huge panes that look out on the Hamersley Range and the tops of them are lost to the low-hanging cloud, isles afloat in humid air. Such peace – strange, strange peace – experiencing what Toby had experienced in death. But for the first time since that reptilian hand scraped clear of the Rift and showed her what had happened to Toby, the doubt wells up like backwash in her throat.

She may as well be sitting back on the verandah of the pub, only now she doesn't have Glen beside her, June or Shrubb, Toby or Lachlan. Instead, she's haloed by strangers. Selfish whingers raving on with the usual racist dross, complaining about how much tax they have to pay, how there are too many Islanders stealing their jobs in the mines. Her dolent eyes rove to drink this all in.

And, worst of all, even here, she's still waiting. Watching the rain fleck harder against the glass, losing sight of the outside, the ground turning to raspberry slurry. Only now, she has no idea what she's waiting for.

But then her thumb flips through the pages of the paperback in her hand. She places *Tourmaline* down on the table. How Toby's fingers brushed hers ever so slightly when they stood side by side, the smile on his face.

Pippa laughs to herself, and all doubt is vanquished. She opens the book to the last page she'd dog-eared. A Māori family comes and sits at the table next to her and she supposes this isn't so bad after all. Not with the Hamersley Range through the window, the softest dapple of rain against the glass, the sound of children laughing.

He returns to the scatter of corrugated iron huts less than twenty-four hours after last seeing them. Glen parks on the side of the gravelly, yellow grassland. Searches the abandoned huts for Shrubb. Can't see him but knows he's here, somewhere.

Last night, after Shrubb asked him to drive to the Bar, they only made it ten k's out of town before Shrubb pointed down a sidetrack, leading off into flatlands, away from the Barite Range. 'Down here.'

'I thought ya wanted to go to ya brother's?' Glen found himself asking, then thought twice about it. 'Shrubby …'

He cleared his voice, said it again, 'Down here.'

It was a long and hair-raising drive, clattering around on the gravel in the dark, until they met back up with the main road and trundled into Nullagine, where Shrubb told him to stop at the pub for more grog. They hit another sidetrack. A great unravelling of spinifex, the stuff of Glen's loveliest dreams. Then, in pitch darkness, the headlights showed some abandoned cattle yards. A ramshackle freckling of little huts station workers had slapped together fifty years ago or so, retooling the junky ripple iron.

He's gunna drink himself to death, Glen thought in the moment. *So what's it matter if ya hurry the process along a bit?*

The temptation was nearly overwhelming, following Shrubb over to one of the huts in the dark, his arms heavy with grog bottles. 'I just need to drink it out,' he explained dimly to Glen over one shoulder, 'Then when I'm done, I'll get ya to take to me to my bro's in the Bar. That okay with you?'

He was almost unaware Shrubb had asked a question. *I'd like to know what your blood feels like on my skin.*

Then coughed. 'Yeah, mate. Sounds good.' He took a moment to look around. 'I mean, not *good*. None of this is *good*. Are ya gunna be alright out here? We're out in the middle'a woop-woop.'

Shrubb gave him a bit of a drunken, impatient look. 'I come here at least a few times a year, mate. I'll be fine.'

Then he saw the inside of the shack Shrubb had been aiming for all this time; a spring mattress with bundles of doonas, a blackened ashtray, even a frypan. Cans of soup. Glen saw all this in the dark, aided only by the moonglow, but his attention snagged the hardest on the sharp-edged things. A piece of wood with a sole nail jutting from it. A length of rusted piping. A red brick.

Glen cast his eyes into furthest night, as if he could sense the titanic heave of the desert from so far away. Hear its gleeful, calling voice.

Shrubb stared at him peevishly. 'I'll be fine, I said.' He went into the hut, started rummaging around. 'Come see me in a couple more days.'

Couldn't do it now. Too incriminating, too obvious. They all saw him drive off with Shrubb from the pub's verandah. Made sense to come back and do it another time. When anything could've happened to the poor bugger, out here and all on his own. The bottles of grog all in a row.

He'd just turned his back to make a hasty escape when Shrubb called, 'And Glenny?' he'd asked, only now did his voice turn croaky. 'Don't tell June where I am.'

And now he's back. Couldn't even wait twenty-four hours.

He could pretend he hasn't been planning this, setting it in motion, since the moment Shrubb asked him to drive over to Marble Bar. Could pretend this hasn't been on his mind the past ten years, since Muswell.

Hands in his pockets, Glen walks towards the scattering of

station tin. The other two huts have fallen inward, rusted frames standing naked, still wrapped with fretting electrical cords. He senses the taxing heat bear down on the back of his neck but keeps on. He stands outside Shrubb's hut and finds his friend so drunk he reels around on his bum, sitting beside a ring of fire-blackened stones.

It was easy to do to Muswell, the little cunt basically had it coming. But here sits his friend. Possibly the best friend Glen's had in a very long time. Since Hannah Parslow. Now he looks at Shrubb, his BO-reek eye-watering, slapped red the same colour as the dirt, the latest bottle by his side, and all Glen can feel is a tide of love for the man. In the way sometimes men allow themselves to love each other. This is true friendship, more than what he'd had with the Parslow girl next door. Surely it couldn't be so easily severed as yanking on one end of that electrical cord over there, so long in the sun it would snap without a sound.

'This is madness,' Glen tells his mate. 'I shouldn't have let ya do this.'

Shrubb looks at him, then scowls angrily. 'I said come back in a few days.'

'I can't let ya do this, Shrubby. Plus, if June ever finds out, she'd throttle me dead.' Glen shakes his head, taking off his wide-brim hat and combing fingers through his thinning grey hair. 'This isn't right.'

Shrubb clears his throat. 'My choice.'

'Sure it is, but are ya makin' the right one?'

Shrubb meets his eyes, some hint of malice in there now. 'Ya still got ya daughter, Glen. She's down there in the city, not like ya seem to wanna spend much time with her.'

Glen clears his throat. 'That's not fair, mate.'

'If Liz was still around, I'd be by her side every wakin' moment. Ya have no fucken clue what this is like. What I carry every day. Not knowin' where she is or what some motherfucker's done to her. Some evil motherfucker. What I'd do to the cunt if I ever knew. If I could just find him.'

'But this shit isn't gunna help.' Glen points down at the bottle, label facing away, as if absolving itself of any responsibility.

'It helps.' Shrubb cackles, his breath akin to a wallop of methylated spirits. 'Trust me, it really does.' He tries to stand, falls back against the hut wall with a loud bang. Glen reaches out to help. 'Git off me,' Shrubb warns him.

Upright, he staggers, nearly stacks it a second time over a pile of corrugated iron sheets crowned with a smooth Bridgestone tyre.

'Let me help,' Glen says. But already, his mind's started to drift.

From here, the spinifex shines off in every knowable direction. He can't sense it now, but he knows how old this soil is beneath his feet. He wonders how it sees the passage of time; linear in the beginning but now all a swirl. How does it see him and Shrubb in this moment, as Shrubb starts to walk away, turning his back? Does it even see Glen? And how can he turn those leviathan eyes his way? Make himself known?

'I don't need ya help,' Shrubb says as he starts away. And Glen sees he's aiming back for his hut now, aiming for another bottle inside. 'Please, just go.'

Glen looks down at the ground. The red brick he saw last night still waiting, tracing out a shape of itself against the crimson dirt. 'But I don't want ya to get hurt.'

'I can look after meself.' Shrubb stops then. If he turned back at that same moment, he would've caught Glen staring down at the brick in an awful trance. He tilts his head, but not enough to find Glen reaching for the ground. 'Just look after June for me. Please, mate?'

The way he says that. *Mate*. That word aches in Glen's chest.

But then he remembers the dark of the desert mushrooming beyond that outcrop of chert, and how he was part of it, a connection in the gristle, in the fibre of its bones. He could trace the slouching of it back to that morass in which single cell squirmers only started to dream themselves into humankind. And by Christ, he wants that so much more. Everything else is insubstantial as smoke, as shadow.

Glen's fingers grip the hard lines of the brick. Mates are few and far between, anyway. What awaits him once he's opened up Shrubb's skull, once he's slicked with hot blood, that is so much more. Fair trade, he reckons.

Fair bloody trade.

It takes a long time walking, a long time thinking about Toby and the cold silence which wrapped around him in the foggy creek water, but now Lachlan finds himself standing in exactly the same spot he was yesterday, right at the mouth of the ravine. At the same hour, too, with the sun lost to the foothills east of the Coongan River, scalding like an infected looking sore in the sky. Lachlan lingers, out of breath, and looks at the dead calf beside the stinking water.

He tries to tell himself he's not a hundred percent sure why he's back, and so soon. Steps closer to the calf, sees its large ribs, bones like stiff paddles in the water, and wonders how it died. Snakebite or heat stroke or maybe the water is poisoned? Doesn't matter. He doesn't need to know how it went, whether it was peaceful and painless.

He needs to see how Toby went. Pippa's description is somehow not enough. He needs to feel it, as she claimed she'd felt it. Needs to know his brother really felt no pain in the end, only that clouding of peace and quiet. The numbness of cold, dirty water.

He's a bit light-headed after chugging on some Woodstock, desperate for liquid courage, and so he staggers a bit, silly and comical as Shrubb used to look, sidestepping the dead calf this time. Weird being here without Pippa. She was like his buffer last night, his shield against what the Rift might decide to show him.

'You know what I want to see,' Lachlan says aloud, as if it's some genie he can summon at will, make demands from.

He winces at the crack in the smooth chert as if he might catch a glimpse of the occupant within but it's too dark. That crack like a splinter in reality. Lachlan stops right in front of it now, noticing there's not a sound in the ravine, no birds singing. Maybe all other living things can smell the intruder and the scent tells them to stay away.

He lingers a moment, regretting this now. He's too drunk for this crazy shit. And now Pippa's gone. *Christ, what the hell am I going to do? How am I going to explain any of this to Mum? She's going to be heartbroken as it is*, he thinks. Then less importantly, *How am I going to keep a fucken servo running until Pippa's back?*

Staring at the Rift, he doesn't know why he straggled out here for answers. Everything that needed to be said has been said. Roll the bloody credits. Walk the fuck away.

But at least there's still this. Him and this. How easily two things can swirl together in the gloaming. His skin roseate like the bends of jasper in the rock face. The four fingers and thumb of a Gila monster, that thing almost-human or almost-more, twangs the catgut powerlines in his chest, and he's catatonic with delight.

He's decided to walk away then, go back and sleep this off, when the hand unsticks itself from the Rift, fitful this time, eager to escape, like watching someone drop their car keys down the side of the driver's seat, and scramble around to re-find their purchase.

Lachlan doesn't shriek, doesn't make a sound, only shivers as the complex, armoured plating touches his skin.

After the fight with Pippa, Toby jumps in his car and bundles down some backroads around Jasper Cliff to clear his head. He finds a lonely creek running with dirty water and steps from his car. There's someone else by the water today. Crouching above the creek, thoughtful and quiet.

Silent until the stranger turns to see Toby by the creek. Smiles and waves.

'No, I've changed my mind!' Lachlan hears himself scream, scrunching his eyes against the vision. 'I don't want to see this!'

Now Toby twists on the spot to find he can barely move, festooned with barbed wire, and when he goes to call out, his jaw is mostly hanging from his face and it produces only a terrible groan. The stranger is out of sight but still whistling casually.

'Still going, are we?' he asks, his faint accent changing the cadence of the question. 'Just won't stay down, will you?'

Toby's rolled a little, and he can see what remains of his car. Its burnt-black husk. The stranger still has that faraway look in his eyes, riding high on the bliss of all this bloodletting. Toby's never been real to him, only ever a fantasy fulfilled. May as well not even be here, and he's almost not.

The stranger kneels beside him now. 'You know, usually I go for the little bitches from town.' He pats the top of Toby's head. 'But that arsehole of yours was something else. Much tighter than any kut I've stuck it to.'

Toby doesn't recall any of this unspeakable detail, but shrieks at the thought.

'Tried me best to stay away from them whores. After the first couple, I tried to stop. But it keeps building, you know? It keeps building inside until it's got to break,' he tells Toby all this as if it's of any consequence anymore. 'I suppose the Cliff will even get its own full-time police station one of these days and then I'll have to look elsewhere to have a bit'a fun, huh?'

Toby peers up at him, gags a little on some broken teeth. Tries to say, 'Please let me go,' but just chokes some more.

'Nothing personal,' the stranger tells him, refusing to meet his eyes. 'Just wrong time,' he straightens and presses the tip of his steel cap boot against the wire in Toby's throat gently, then applies pressure. 'Wrong fucken place.'

Toby tries to say something more but then hears his larynx make an awful crunching sound.

'Go to sleep now, sweet boy,' the Dutchman says, baring his teeth with strange pleasure. 'Go the fuck to sleep.'

Lachlan doesn't feel the occupant release him, only finds himself snapped back into the ravine with the click of fingers. He must've been screaming the entire time the vision flickered before his eyes and not been able to hear it. And now he does, listening in horror to the pathetic, guttural sound he's projecting up against the cracked face of red rock.

Now released, Lachlan tries to fathom being back in the ravine alone, watching the hand from the Rift scrape back into the chert interior. He rubs at his throat where he felt the truck driver's footrest, pushing the barb wire deeper into his skin, or Toby's. He stands there staring at the hot rock face, trembling so hard he thinks his ankles might give way. The wizened mouth in the cliff that won't speak. Won't answer any of his questions, can't soothe the petrified look on his face now.

'That's not what you showed Pippa,' he mutters.

So which one is the truth? Lachlan thinks, backing away and rubbing frantically at where the scaly hand seized him. Toby falling into the creek, or Toby with his throat stepped on by that mad bastard?

One or the other must be the lie. Lachlan turns and flees across rocky ground, not quite running. He's still shaking hard and fears his legs might go rubbery under him, leave him flailing in the dirt. An arsenal of birds meets him at the mouth of the ravine once he's free.

He halts to watch a falcon swoop down and snatch a cricket out of the cooling air.

Or they could both be lies.

Because both couldn't be the truth.

There's a seething rage inside him, now he's back on the edge of the grasslands. He peers back past the dead calf in the water but from here he can't see the black lightning rod of the crack in the Rift. He almost bolts back in there to drive his arm into that crack to snatch back at whatever furled within, dragging the truth out of it, out into the cool night sky.

But then he recalls all those missing paper faces on the wall of the deli back in town. What makes him so special that he deserves the truth more than anyone else here?

That scaly oracle behind the rock face – what if it showed him and Pippa what they needed to see? After all, it has saved Pippa; Lachlan knew this as soon as he read her letter, feeling the paper warp under his sweaty touch. She's free, in a way he isn't, and might never be now.

Lachlan rubs at his throat, where he feels the truck driver's boot driving deeper into his little brother's neck again, and he turns back to the grasslands, the sky now a strange violet in the near dark.

He'd wanted the truth, but the truth was a luxury afforded to none here in Jasper Cliff.

11

He doesn't believe in this hocus pocus, spooky bullshit. Not really.

And he would've thought Lachlan was too smart to believe it. Well, maybe he didn't believe in it until a couple of nights ago. Now he's a believer, that's for sure. Glen can see how that belief has broken him already.

He wanders down to the pub around ten, wondering if he's made the right decision. After all, lazy days on the verandah at Pip's now just won't be the same. Not with June and Pippa gone, and Shrubb's headless, handless body deep in the red dirt of the grasslands between here and Nullagine. Still, it isn't him that got Shrubby back on the grog. Can thank Lachlan for that one.

Maybe ya messed up bad this time? Glen passes the payphone now, dripping with the spray of a misguided shire sprinkler.

But he knows that's not true. Not as he remembers how he reeled and swayed, insides all swishing, after he finished off Shrubb. Took the hacksaw to his wrists and throat and plopped the hands and head in a garbage bag, so the body wasn't so easily identifiable, if it was ever found at all. Then buried him in the cold shadow of that unfilled water tank, along with his empty whiskey bottles.

Once the legwork was done, Glen could take what he wanted. Set out into the spread of Kingsmill's mallees, a pious fool distant as a single star upon the scrunched back of the grasslands. That first time, after he'd dispatched Muswell, he'd sensed the black enormity of the desert reach to obscure the night, but this time, Glen sensed even more. This land red and crowning from primordial sea and, already, too many years to count back, Glen was stumbling across its flank into that cascade of millennium after millennium.

Peering up, he sees Lachlan alone outside the pub, and Glen calls barleys on these thoughts. Needs to appear human again for the only human about. Then he sees the bottle of Woodstock at Lachlan's feet and starts getting Shrubby flashbacks. The sad look in his eyes as Glen sawed through his neck, though he was already dead, skull broken inward.

'Can't say I approve,' Glen sings out, trying to be funny. 'Especially when ya don't offer me any.'

But Lachlan's far from laughing. He drinks and Glen draws his camp chair close to ask him what's wrong. Even then, Lachlan doesn't answer, only stares down the main street at where Aunty Belle's already neatly established herself under the ghost gum.

He tips the last of the bottle up to drain what remains, then looks at Glen with a terror which rattles him to his core. Not even Muswell looked like this, even as he felt the first blow of the star picket, even as he felt his uprooted teeth bounce against the back of his throat.

'You know, surprisingly, the wi-fi isn't so bad here?' Lachlan says, his eyes searching for something, or nothing at all, far away in the distance. 'Maybe I can learn sign language on some YouTube tutorials?'

Glen nods up at the roof across the road. 'Can thank the community centre for that one. The shire knocked up some kinda booster for it a coupla years ago. Not that half of us in the Cliff are all that eager to be checkin' our emails every five minutes.'

Lachlan doesn't laugh. Just lists there, drooping like he might sink through the material of his chair and ooze to the ground.

Glen only has to ask him what the matter is a few more times before Lachlan breaks. He tears up but he doesn't cry, as if the fear is paralysing some of the muscles in his face. He then lets it all out in a surfeit that leaves Glen frowning. He was rubbing Lachlan's shoulder in consolation but then feels himself withdraw his hand, fearing the young bloke's completely lost his fucken marbles.

Lachlan explains how he and Pippa went out to the Rift, describes the scaled hand which shot from the crack in the rock face and grabbed Pippa. Then how she fitted, eyes rolling around, and what she claims to have seen in her mind's eye when that hand seized her.

Glen remembers them taking Shrubb out there, then returning in a fluster, but Glen had been too worried about June at the time to pay much notice. He'd never once thought any of this nonsense might actually be real. Just another ghost story. More than a few out in this neck of the woods.

Now Lachlan goes into the pub, leaving Glen alone on the verandah. He wonders if the young bloke might have some mental health problem. They're always going on about it on the ABC, saying how bad it is in young people these days. Had to be something like that; he simply couldn't have seen what he'd claimed to have seen.

Lachlan returns with another Woodstock, cracks the lid.

He's already turnin' into Shrubby.

Glen thinks if the young bloke keeps going this way, he might be able to get him off into the spinifex a bit. Use a brick on the back of his head, cut and saw, and then Glen can drift high and swirl with the red jasper in the faces of the foothills again. Much sooner than he anticipated.

Once every ten years simply isn't enough.

After a few more mouthfuls, Lachlan explains that he went back last night to the Rift. After a few drinks. That same hand emerged from the rock and grabbed him. Now he describes what he saw, completely different to what Pippa claimed she'd seen. He's not making any sense.

'Don't think I'm followin',' Glen tells him, trying to soften his voice, convey some crumb of understanding. 'It showed youse two different things?'

'Very different. Two different stories, or series of events, I guess you'd say. But one has to be the truth, right?' Lachlan asks, his breath smelling like a spirits shelf. 'I know which one I'd rather believe.'

Glen's leathery hand finds his shoulder again, squeezes. 'Mate, this has got me bloody worried. This all sounds … so …'

Batshit.

But Lachlan goes on, 'I don't know what it is. And I don't want to know either. But it's old, I could feel that when it touched me. It can see so much more than us, see out so much further. It sees these things and then tells the stories. I guess, to whoever is willing to listen. To *see*.' He drinks some more. 'It tells the stories of the lost.'

Now it's Glen's turn to look afraid. He thinks of Muswell, Shrubb. Only he knew, surely. What happened to them. What he'd done.

'The stories I guess that might fall through the cracks.' Lachlan jabs his finger down the main street. 'All'a them on that fucken wall. It knows what happened to them. It has their stories.' Then points at Aunty Belle. 'Her daughter, it knows what happened to her too. June and Shrubb's. It knows it all, Glen.'

'It can't,' Glen hears himself say, with dying hope. 'None of this can be real, son. I'm scared all'a this is in your head.'

Lachlan glares at him furiously a moment, then quells his rage with another drink. 'Well, there's an easy way to tell if that's the case or not.' His hand judders as he places the bottle back on the green concrete below. 'Go out there and take a look for yourself.'

He's planning on doing just that when he looks up and sees June approach along the footpath. It's taken most of the day to talk Lachlan down, get him away from the drink. Then help him into the pub, back to his bed, where Lachlan floundered and was asleep within seconds, while Glen was still trying to give him hollow reassurances.

Watching June stop at Aunty Belle's tree, a short recess in which the two converse, Glen quickly sits in his camp chair to make it look like he's been here all day and isn't about to rush out to the Rift, to see if Lachlan and Pippa's batshit crazy stories aren't entirely batshit crazy after all.

When June finally keeps on down the footpath, sidestepping a sprinkler which the shire workers have left running all day, he tries his best for a smile. His best has always been sufficient, fooling all around, lulling them into the falsity that he's harmless as a fly.

'My dear friend,' Glen says, watching her step onto the flaking green paint, coming away from the concrete in patches. 'I really didn't expect to see ya again so soon. The other night was so rough. On us all but you and Shrubby most of all.'

'Where is he?' she asks point blank.

By *he*, Glen assumes she means Lachlan. 'Sleepin' it off. He's been hittin' the grog a bit hard, in truth. Battlin' with his conscience, I suspect.'

June nods, and Glen looks at the duffel bag she has swung across one shoulder.

'Goin' somewhere?'

'I think ya know where.'

That gets his spine tingling. *What does that mean exactly?*

When he got down to Shrubb's windpipe with the hacksaw, there was a gasping sound. At first, he wondered if Shrubb could somehow, inexplicably, still be alive after the beating he'd taken with the red brick. But as Glen kept sawing, he realised it was just an evacuation of air, the last of it fleeing his body.

'Ya didn't take Shrubb to the Bar, did ya?' June asks.

He can't hurt her too, not out here in the open. Dead as the Cliff is most days, Glen knows he still can't dismantle someone on the main street, out the front of the pub for anyone to see.

'Even as he said it, asked ya to take him to his brother's in Marble Bar the other night, part'a me already knew what he had planned. Part'a me knew he wasn't gunna make it.' June lets the duffel thump to the ground. 'Lived with the bugger twenty years, mind you. I know how he thinks. Now he's started drinkin', he's not gunna stop for a while.'

She doesn't know, Glen realises, the tension in his throat relenting. *Of course, she doesn't. How could she?*

But this thought is quickly followed by, *But the Rift might.*

'I'm really sorry, June-bug,' Glen says. 'I did honestly think he wanted to go to his brother's in the Bar. Otherwise, I wouldn't have agreed to drive him.'

'Where did he get ya to drop him off?'

Think fast.

'Made me turn around after we got out of sight.' His lies flow like water. 'Once you and Pip couldn't see. We argued for a bit. Right there on the side of the road. Kept tellin' him if he wanted to keep drinkin', he could just bloody walk.' Glen sighs. 'Then I thought better of it. Didn't really want him walkin' along the side'a the road at night. He wanted to go to Nullagine. So that's where I took him.'

She nods. 'Thought as much. Somewhere he could keep drinkin' without bein' told off. That town's fast dyin' away, but you watch. Thanks to the miners, the pub will be the last thing to go. I rang his brother this mornin' and he'd seen no sign. We agreed to go lookin' for the silly bastard.'

Glen nods, fakes his best guilty look. 'I really am sorry, June.'

'Not ya fault. Ya've always been a good friend to him. Him and me both.' She nods, scoops up her duffel again which he can tell from her grimace is hurting her shoulder. 'Thank you. For lookin' out for him as long as ya did.'

Glen rattles the keys in his pocket. 'Let me drive ya.'

But she lifts an open hand to silence him. 'S'alright. Doris Neave and her son are gunna drive me. They're hittin' the road tonight for a funeral in the city anyway. S'all sorted.'

He settles back into his seat, a failed launch, like watching a foal try stand on stilty legs and collapse back down. Can't help but feel disappointed. If she'd agreed to a lift, he could've taken her out into the spinifex. Closely, riding on the back of disappointment, comes this sadness. June going now too. Jasper Cliff is falling apart before his very eyes.

'I'll call in a few days,' she tells him. 'Keep ya updated.'

'I'd appreciate that. To know you're safe.'

She looks at the pub grimly. 'Look after that boy. I understand why he did what he did, doesn't mean I have to forgive him for it but.'

'He's a work-in-progress.'

'Aren't we all?' she asks. 'And don't stress about Shrubby either. Ya know he does this at least once a year. Gets a taste for the piss again and then disappears for a bit. Unfortunately, it's usually me who's gotta go out and drag his arse home.' She smiles a little to think of him, while Glen can only picture him headless and handless now, the bloodied stumps of his wrists and neck. 'Don't you worry, I'll bring him home.'

Glen returns her smile. 'Please do.' And he truly means it when he confesses, 'I miss him already.'

She's gone then, hauling the duffel at her side. Not just a hint of heat on the wind when it blows, but a claw of it. He waits until she's out of sight before fetching his keys and making for the Triton parked by the bowsers.

He finds the big chunk of red rock Lachlan mentioned when he explained where the Rift was and Glen slows the ute alongside it, then hangs there peering down the sand track, ahead and then through the back pane.

'I must be goin' batshit meself to even bother with this,' he says aloud.

As he kills the engine and feels the aircon die, the sweat instantly pricks along his brow. From under the driver's seat, he retrieves the same hacksaw he used on Shrubb last night. Considers it a moment blankly and then steps into a glorious crimson swell of sky, the foothills boiling over the top of each other. Only last night he stumbled, Shrubb's blood stuck to his skin, and walked the ages back towards the birth of creation. Slitted eyelids of jasper in such hills remember that birth so clearly, and now so does Glen.

He stomps out into the hummock grassland a bit, kicking through Sturt peas and cow pats, and almost turns back after a kilometre or so. *This is stupid. No one knows what ya did to Muswell or Shrubby. Especially some lizard thing livin' behind some bloody rocks.* It spits in the face of everything he's ever assumed about the world, shatters any logic. *Couldn't be real. Just couldn't be.*

So he wonders why he keeps walking until he finds the dead calf. The reek precedes it, warns him of its presence, ribs like slender ghost fingers all gnarled, as if they might close around something substantial. He trembles a little to look at the ravine, see how it appears much as Lachlan had described it. And Shrubb before him.

He perseveres with his doubt. Can't be real.

Still, on the off-chance it might be, he has to be sure. He clamps his nostrils closed to sidestep the puddle of putrid water, jostling the hacksaw around in one fist a little nervously. *Ridiculous, fucken bonkers, this is.* There's just hot red stones and some wirewood. Patches of loam. Not even any animals, no birds. Nothing that could've seen so far away, as to witness him bashing Muswell's brains from his skull, severing Shrubb's hands at the stubborn wrists.

He sees it now, can understand why they call it the Rift. It's mostly bisected by a huge crack that's wound its way down the rock face. Glen catches his breath, wasn't anticipating how beautiful it would be, the threads of red jasper in the chert bending back over each other. He stumbles before it, caught up with the red rock in throes of confluent passion.

Then, once close enough, there's a soft scraping within and Glen has to reassess everything he's ever taken for granted in this world. Because this couldn't be real – no fucking way – and yet he's watching it happen before his very eyes. Once jacked on the heady contours of the ravine, now Glen tries to thrash away. But he's too late, and he watches the hand, caiman scaly – but much bigger than any fucken caiman he's ever seen – latch onto his wrist—

Glen looks down to see the brick in his hand but now he's clearer than he's felt since that last ecstatic bloodletting. Doesn't let the doubt dribble back in; shoves away any inconvenient empathy. And he lobs the brick straight into the back of Shrubb's head.

Hot blood soaks through that ratty cap instantly and Glen quickly swipes the brick off the ground and straightens. Shrubb face down and not making a sound and Glen wonders if the job's already done. But he can't stumble out into the grasslands yet, feel the components of himself joining with the greater components of the land, unless he gets a sweat going.

So he hits Shrubb in the back of the head again. And it's better than with Muswell. Messier. Glen strikes again and again, and he can already sense himself getting clearer, as if he's seeing himself in the mirror for the first time. Yeah, that's what this is. He's been invisible his entire life, but now the land sees him, truly sees him, he can see himself. Grunting happily above his friend's lifeless body.

He just can't be sure if the land is looking at him with a satiated expression, or a horrified one.

Softly, the lizard fingers release him and Glen's back in the ravine, no longer hauling the brick back with a crooked arm for another blow. Can still remember how Shrubb's head was spilling out a blood omelette when he was finally done.

It knows, Glen thinks in a panic. *How can it possibly know that?*

The hand starts to retract and Glen's surprised at his own agility as he finds himself snatching it by the wrist. The reptilian limb struggles against his hold a moment, and this close, clutching the hand against his hip now, Glen can see that the hand is attached to an arm, and that arm is attached to a shoulder, but the rest is overshadowed by the depths of the Rift.

'I can't let ya show that to anyone else.'

It's easier to do this, because it's covered in scales. It's not a friend, like Shrubb was. And definitely not human. Glen uses all his strength to drag a bit more of the arm out. The caking perspiration has doused most of his body by the time he realises he's not going to get much more into the clear, so he rests the hacksaw against the elbow joint. Grinds his teeth. Works the handle.

A rasping, see-saw sound, like listening to someone cut

greenwood. Blood runs from the lizard armour, and he may as well be amputating a crocodile's diseased foot. But no sound from whatever this forearm is connected to, no scream of pain or horror.

Glen keeps at his work, but glances at the Rift in terrible wondering. 'What in all the holy hell are you?'

Hard yakka once he reaches the bone, and he hacks and hacks, and it's much tougher going than when he removed Shrubb's head and hands, the ligaments and sinew more rigid than Shrubb's had been. Still, not a whimper from within the crack of red stone.

Finally, he saws down to the last scrap of scaly flesh and severs it completely, revealing a clean protrusion of elbow bone. What's left of the arm slowly retreats inside the Rift, almost gently, and Glen's left there standing, hacksaw in one hand, the separated reptilian forearm in the other.

'That's what ya get for bein' a fucken tattletale,' he spits.

He turns to watch the fingers of the hand which showed him the truth of what he'd done to Shrubb slowly close in on themselves. Realises there's four digits and a thumb; way too human now, too close for comfort. He rummages his way out of the ravine until he's past the dead calf and he's back into the crimson-lit grasslands.

He looks at the forearm again. *Fuck am I supposed to do with this thing?* Glen wonders. *Feed it to Dave Sedden's dog?*

He decides it's safer to bury it. As he moves off again, he stumbles and cuts a wonky path into the spinifex, then stops at a random spot, gets down on his knees and starts scratching away at the surface of the red soil with the claw of one hand, dropping the caiman-scaled forearm at his side so he can paw away at the loams. Once he's down far enough, he shuffles the forearm in and quickly closes the scarlet tide back over with his shoe, as if burying a difficult memory. He'd bury it deeper if the ground wasn't starting to blur before his eyes, swaying this way and that. He stands to dust himself off, picks the hacksaw back up and lets it tap against his knee, wet with lizard blood.

Once he's upright again, he swoons. The grassland reticulates around him in hazy circles. The heat has cooked a pink burn across his forehead and he rakes at the rush of sweat beading from his face. He guesses cutting off that lizard-thing's forearm must've taken more out of him than he thought.

It takes some time to straggle back to the Triton and it's that fierce, reddest red of sky just before darkness, when the heat of the day is compressed along the Coongan River, reality warped. He almost slumps against the cab, a solid dose of blood whacking against the white paintjob.

'The shit?' Glen mutters.

He looks down and, at first, can't tell where so much blood has come from, saturating a patch of his clothes. Now the nausea sets in, a food blender firing up inside his stomach as he opens the back door and lets the saw clatter onto the floor. Still spinning, Glen imagines a bunch of forensics boffins going over the handsaw, finding traces of Shrubb's blood. But not just Shrubb's blood. Their tests would also come back for something reptilian, but ultimately unidentifiable.

Before he can yank open the driver's door, he hunches and vomits a little in the dirt. Then stares at it pooling and wonders if this is the land's punishment for some reason, for cutting the forearm from the intruder, the trespasser, or whatever Lachlan had called it.

He's just spat the last of the spew out and streaked more blood across the bonnet – maybe his, maybe the intruder's – and looks over the bonnet just in time to see the mangiest dingo he's ever seen sprint across the gravel in front of him. A tiny racer darting away, a bit of a limp to the bitch's stride.

He has to blink a couple of times to convince himself what he's seeing is actually happening. It could just as easily be some kind of vertigo-induced delusion. Fast on the heels of the dingo is the biggest bloody dog Glen's ever seen in the bush. A Bernese mountain dog, he thinks they're called. Must've fled Jasper Cliff or Nullagine or Marble Bar years ago and gone mad and feral out here on its own.

Glen watches it lumber hungrily after the skinny dingo but he can tell it has no hope of ever catching the bitch. No hope in hell. This all transpires in less than ten seconds and then they're both gone into the grasslands again and that's that. He hangs there, the grasslands whipping themselves into another spin, trying to swallow the next welling of vomit, and he gets the sense the chase has been going on for some time now. Those two locked in a perpetual state of pursuit and conflict, ephemeral, gaunt and starving mongrels. One might never catch the other – only the chase continues. A battle of fading wills.

Glen collapses behind the steering wheel and cranks the engine. No hope, he thinks as he drives away.

12

He wishes he could conjure a great and tenebrous beast into the sky. And in wishing, Lachlan can almost see it. Can see its immense, ursine back breaking through the stiff crust of the Coongan Riverbed, rising to slouch across the foothills. Such a beast of towering stature might stub its toe on an awkward little stone like Jasper Cliff.

He wishes it out into the world, to do away with all the horror he's been so blind to most of his life, until he came to this place. Until he saw all the flapping faces of the missing on the deli wall. He wishes up a beast to scrape the human scum from the surface of the pond. If only wishes could manifest fur and teeth and claws.

Sitting with his laptop at the bar, still buzzing after how much he's had to drink earlier that morning, Lachlan scrolls for a while, sweating profusely on the stool. After he creates a Facebook page for Toby – and a GoFundMe to raise money to help with his search – Lachlan looks elsewhere. Pages of countless missing people on the Crime Stoppers website, and that is just this state alone. How many across the country? The world? Toby is just another fluttering face on the deli wall now.

He's posted as many details about Toby's car as he can, down to the bloody VIN number. Says the vehicle was last spotted in the Jasper Cliff area but could be as far away as Nullagine or Marble Bar. He also gives a description of the Dutch truck driver. Doesn't say too much but asks if anyone has seen him or his truck, can they please get in contact; this man might have information pertinent to Toby Bowman's whereabouts.

In an attempt to clear his thoughts, he moves on to YouTube. He's just finished a thirty-minute tutorial on Auslan for beginners, when he peers at the open pub door, expecting the warm lick of dying sunlight. For a moment, he sees Glen silhouetted in that doorway, dark as a phantom.

'Hope I'm not interrupting?'

Lachlan blinks until he's staring at Connor standing in the doorway, not Glen as he'd feared for some reason. Connor's strangling a cap in his hands and he's no longer in uniform so it's no wonder Lachlan hadn't recognised him at first with his scuffed camo shorts and T-shirt stretched at the neck.

He raises his eyebrows. 'Mind if I come in?'

Lachlan closes the lid on the laptop. 'How long you been creeping there?'

'Not long.' He makes some signs in the air. 'Auslan?'

'Only just started.'

'Half the kids in school here had problems with hearing. Suppose it could've helped knowing it back in the day.' He clears his throat and looks up and down the main street, now slowly darkening, and Lachlan doesn't think he's ever seen someone more uncomfortable with how he fidgets on the spot, continues to wring the life from his black cap.

'Sorry. Yeah, come in. Pippa's not here, so I'm looking after the joint for the time being.'

The boards groan with Connor's weight. He settles his stiff cap on the bar. 'How long's that for? Pippa not here, I mean?'

Lachlan shrugs. 'For the foreseeable future, I guess. She needs some time for herself. After everything that's happened, I'm happy to give her that.'

Connor nods and looks at the empty grog shelves along the wall. 'You had the same look on your face everyone gives me, you know? When you first saw me standing there just now. You looked shit-scared.'

I thought you were Glen, he thinks strangely, because Glen has never really done anything to make him so afraid.

'Seeing a cop on your doorstep often has that effect.' Connor smiles bitterly. 'The perpetual bearer of bad news.'

'I guess if you had bad news for me, about Toby, you'd be in uniform.'

He nods. 'That I would be.'

'So what's up then?' Lachlan swivels a little on his stool, careful not to lose his groggy footing. 'Just home for a quick visit?'

'*Home*?' he asks, the bitterness returning. 'As if this place could ever be called *home*. Do you have any idea how many lives this fucken town has swallowed up?'

'I'm starting to get an idea.'

Connor finally builds the courage to meet Lachlan's eyes. 'Aunty June isn't right about a lot of stuff. She's too often blinded by her own grief.' He drags in a deep breath. 'But she is right about one thing. This town invested a lot in me, and I don't want to let it down any longer. As much as it gives me the bloody heebie-jeebies. Whenever I drive back down that main street, I get the shivers like someone just walked over my grave.'

Lachlan remembers the feeling of that shadow rumbling in the corner of his vision that first morning in the Cliff. Turns out maybe he and Connor aren't all that different.

'This fucking job,' Connor goes on. 'I already feel a hundred years old. It's like pushing shit uphill every day only to watch it slowly roll back over you.' He rests both open hands on the bar, then slowly closes them into fists. 'But that doesn't mean I'm ever gunna stop pushing.'

Lachlan raises his eyebrows. 'Okay,' he says. 'So um, what does that mean? What are you going to do?'

He strums his fingers on the bar top now. 'I guess it means you'll be seeing a whole lot more of me around here. You all will.'

Lachlan sinks a bit to hear this. 'Well, those of us who are left. Shrubb took off on a bender and June went after him. And Pip's taking a break. For now, it's just Glen and me.'

That pitch-black phantom lingering in the open doorway again. Lachlan tries to shake this spectre away for good but only spins with the grog-dizzies.

Connor smiles at him, not unkindly. 'There's a whole lot more to Jasper Cliff than this bloody pub, mate.'

Lachlan laughs. 'Of course, sorry. Yeah. I've had a drink or two.'

Now Connor laughs, whacks him on the shoulder. 'All good. Can't blame you for that.' His eyes soften. 'Actually, I thought I might ask about your brother. You said he was spending a lot of time out in the hills by the river? Bit of a keen bushwalker, so Pippa tells me.'

Lachlan nods, daring to hope.

'Thought you and I might go for a bit of a cruise around and take a look? If you feel up to it? What do you reckon?'

Lachlan checks out the open pub door. 'Pretty dark out.'

'Unofficially, working out here, I'm on call seven days. This might be the only time I can give you this week.'

'No, no. That's awesome,' he says and drops from his stool. 'Let's go. Thank you.'

Connor halts a moment, watching him closer. 'Just, um, don't chunder in my car, will you?'

'No vomit.' Lachlan smiles. 'It's a promise.'

He crosses the creaky pub boards behind Connor to join him on the verandah. His head's still drubbing from the whiskey and Coke, every muscle strained and achy. But he's not sure it'll keep him away from going back to the drink. The deli might be shut for the night but it opens at nine o'clock tomorrow morning. He can see every day he remains will be a struggle but he guesses that's okay; he'd like to think he's stronger than most might think.

'Like I said, June's wrong about some stuff, but she was right the other day. I think there's more I can do for this place.' Connor stares down the main street now, towards the ghost gum. 'I spent most of the night back at the Bar, put out the feelers about Aunty Belle's daughter. It's already considered a cold case, you know. Can only hope that if I keep putting the pressure on, bit by bit, we might one day start to get answers.'

'Imagine waiting all these years,' Lachlan says, now gripping the verandah post to keep himself from going down face-first, 'And still having no answers at all.'

Connor glances back at him. 'Ask you something?'

'Can I stop you?'

'The sign language thing.' He shrugs. 'Why bother? Seems like a lot of bother for someone you've really only just met.'

Lachlan looks down at the ghost gum. Aunty Belle left hours ago but she spends so much time under there it's like an imprint of her remains beneath the dangling foliage after she goes home for the night. 'One day, I think I'd like to talk to her. But, you know, a proper conversation. Not like me talking at her and not understanding what she's saying back,' he explains. 'And when that day comes, I want to be able to understand what she has to say. I want to know the right things to say in return.'

Connor smiles a little with that. 'You never met her daughter. Smartest kid around. She could've been anything she wanted to be. But she knew what this town needed and was set on being just that.'

'And what was that exactly? What did this town need?'

'A believer.' His smile warm, but only lasts a moment longer in the dark. 'She wanted to be a lawyer. She'd chew your ear off for hours about Native Title. Treaties. She was only a couple of years older than me but I always looked up to her. Think that's why I joined the force. Thought I could make a difference. Change things.'

'You still can.'

'I don't know.' Connor looks down at the Nissan Patrol parked by the bowsers, must be his personal car. 'It's like every chance this town gets, something snatches it away.'

Lachlan swallows the taste of bourbon, but steels himself through the nausea. 'It's not gone, though. Not really,' he says. 'Not if we snatch it back.'

He peers down the road, not a hint of headlights arriving in town. And he wonders if he'll see the Dutch truck driver again. Hear the hissing of the Kenworth's brakes and then listen for those monstrous tyres rolling into Jasper Cliff, crunching over the blue metal. Maybe the one who stole his little brother's life. Maybe not. He's not even sure what he'd do if he saw the truck driver again. Supposes he has plenty of time to think about it. The truckie could be back for a fill of diesel tomorrow, or a month from now. A year.

Never again.

'You reckon we can find them?' Connor asks, the fear finally rattling in his voice, as the hot night presses in on all sides.

At first, Lachlan thinks he's referring to Pippa, June and Shrubb. But then realises he means the flappy faces on the deli wall. 'Maybe,' Lachlan says.

He looks for the Barite Range, can only just make it out sketched against the darkness. He might even return to the Rift tomorrow. Again and again, to feel that scaly hand grip his, until he knows how they all vanished. Toby. Elizabeth Shrubb. Aunty Belle's daughter. He'll take whatever it can throw at him, endure the bloody horrors playing out in his mind's eye.

That's if it shows you the truth, he thinks.

Maybe it's not so much the truth that matters, Lachlan finally decides. But the searching.

Connor nods and hits the electronic lock and the Patrol's indicators flash. 'Well, either way,' he says, and they both start towards the four-wheel drive, 'no harm in looking.'

Glen watches red tail-lights escaping out the other side of town as he pulls up beside the bowsers. He doesn't hit the brakes fast enough, so his ute noses the chain-link fence between the servo and the vacant house next door before coming to a halt.

'Christ's sake,' he mutters aloud but his voice sounds miles away.

Resisting the urge to vomit again, Glen wrenches at the door handle and spills out onto the bitumen, noticing stripes of blood across the dash and windshield. A dark puddle of it warm on the driver's seat. 'Lachie?' he calls out, voice jagged and stuttering. 'Where are ya, Lach?'

Now he's on the skillet-hot ground by the ute, he hears something like a rat or possum scuttle by, tiny claws spidering over the tarmac. Glen crouches to check under the Triton and finds nothing but darkening street.

'Think there's somethin' out here with me, Lach,' he says.

When he turns to the pub now, he finds it completely vacated. The two empty chairs still set up as if waiting for familiar bums to fill them. *You did that,* he thinks somewhere in the foggy corners of his muddled brain as he manages to straighten his achy knees and stumble to his feet. *It was a good thing you had here – maybe the best thing you ever had – and you ruined it.*

Glen wishes he could feel bad about it, for what he did to Ricky Muswell. For disappearing Shrubb and renting divisions between his little verandah family. But now the moon has hovered up above the Barite Range and night is nearly upon him, he knows it was all worth it. The warping of the land through him after he was covered in Shrubb's blood; there was nothing so dissolute he wouldn't do to have that again. He would empty every chair in his life if needed.

Whatever's out here with him in the dark scuttles right by his feet this time. Comes within inches of his boots. Glen yanks his sore knee away. 'Git fucked!'

He crawls away from the side of the ute, snatches a hold of the verandah beam and peers back at the half-parked, half-crashed vehicle, checking for what might be dashing over the tarmac around the bowers. His eyes settle on the shocking amount of blood inside the ute cab instead. *What the hell?* he thinks. *There wasn't that much blood on the handsaw. There wasn't even that much on me.*

When Glen looks down, he's caked from the waist down in gore, oil-black in the moonlight. 'Where did all this come from?' He stumbles through the open doorway into the pub.

It's completely dark inside as Lachlan must've forgotten to turn on the lights and he calls out again, 'Lachie? Ya still here, mate?' His stomach swirls and flips over, the liquor shelves jumping back and forth against the wall. His heart clamours madly to remember the sound of whatever was just scampering around at his feet outside. He glances back over his shoulder to quickly check nothing with claws has followed him inside.

'Not feelin' too flash here, Lach. Might need a hand.'

Then recalls cutting off the reptilian forearm, watching its fingers curl into the scaly palm. *Get it? I need a hand.*

He laughs, delirious. Once he realises there's no one else in here, Glen starts to unbutton his shirt, long before he reaches the hall down to the showers. On some level, he understands it's better if Lachlan isn't here; that way, he won't see Glen covered in blood and demand an explanation. Another lucky break. But he won't have long. He'll need to wash and dump these clothes drenched in lizard blood before Lachlan gets back.

And get away from whatever the hell is following him.

He nearly makes it to the communal showers when the next bout of vomit singes his throat and then drips feebly onto the ground at his feet, like a baby spew. Must be less than a few metres from the cool tiles of the bathroom but he knows he's not going to make it, not with the pub spinning away under him. Instead, he crashes through the nearest door, into one of the guestrooms kept constantly made-up by Pippa, though a little dusty.

He collapses on the double bed, his sweaty brow thwacking the pillow. 'Just need to rest a sec,' he says, muffled into the scent of mothballs. 'Just gimme a sec here.'

But the scampering is the clearest he's heard so far now. He is only moments from slipping away into the dark when his eyes spring back open. The scurrying takes its time coming down the wooden boards in the hallway. Glen gently rolls to one side, the mattress already soaked and hot under him, and sees he's left the guestroom door wide open.

'Please God, no.'

Moonlight will unveil his pursuer. His punisher. He can hear its claws long and unyielding, surely leaving deep scores in the wood grain. He swallows the taste of his bile and can't help but wonder if this is the price he must pay. Not for what he did to the intruder within the Rift, but for Ricky Muswell and Shrubb. Couldn't take something like that – experience a thing as eclipsing as that – and not give something back in return.

Glen watches as the severed forearm dashes into the open doorway. He only sawed it off less than half an hour earlier but it's agile as a ferret hunting mice now it's detached from whatever elbow joint had once supported it. Still, it drips hardly any blood where Glen hacked away and it pauses at the base of the guest bed, covered in a fine sleeve of red dirt after being buried on the edge of town.

'I'm sorry, okay?' he blabbers, hooking the sheets up around him as if this would be any kind of shield against what's coming for him. 'It was nothin' personal.'

When the severed, scaly hand clambers up the foot of the bed, Glen starts to scream. He realises, vaguely, he's never heard a scream like it before. But then again, he supposes he never gave Ricky Muswell a chance to scream. Shrubb either. He hit them hard in the back of the head before they could embarrass themselves like this.

It is a mercy the intruder's forearm seems unwilling to allow as it latches onto his face.

Glen wakes, wailing like a child scared of what's rustling under the bed. A nightmare. Only a nightmare. He tries to catch his breath as he rolls over in the guest bed, blinking the stinging tears out of his eyes. Nothing in the doorway now, scampering after him. Must've imagined it all. Thank God, he imagined it all.

It's only once he reaches for the edge of the mattress, still intent on dragging himself towards the showers Pippa let him use when the water was off at his place, that he peers down at the bloodied stump under him and finally sees what has been concealed to him since he left the Rift earlier. What he has been so blind to all this time.

Funny, how something can be right in front of your eyes for so long, and the only reason you haven't seen it is because it's too horrible to come to terms with.

Too horrible to believe.

They get back late and by the time Connor has brought the Patrol to a halt on the intersection of the main street and the road back out of Jasper Cliff, Lachlan has sobered up quite a bit.

He is expecting a rush of despair now he can no longer feel the whiskey charging through his veins but finds himself dangerously content instead. While they'd found nothing but a bag of rubbish and a dead eagle traversing the backroads, wriggling like worms through the hills along the Coongan River, Lachlan had been glad just to watch the country rolling by in Connor's headlights.

Once Lachlan steps from the four-wheel drive, still a bit wobbly, he peers in at Connor looking dejected behind the steering wheel. 'Thank you for that. I appreciate it more than I can probably articulate.'

This doesn't lift Connor. 'Don't have anything to thank me for. Not yet.'

'But I will,' he says and tries his hardest for a smile. 'I'm sure of it. And soon.'

Connor nods, smiles faintly back. 'If I don't have any new information by the weekend, I'll come back out on Sunday night. Same again?'

Lachlan nods. 'I'll make sure Glen can watch the servo this time.'

'Sounds like a plan.' Now Connor peers down the main street towards the pub, past Aunty Belle's ghost gum. 'Are you sure you want to be dropped off here? Hop back in a sec. I'll take you all the way back to the servo.'

'It's fine. It's not far and I like to walk.'

Connor doesn't say it but the fear is plain in his eyes; this might not be the place to go wandering around by yourself at night. Whatever ravenous jaws haunt this town would surely be far too tempted to snatch you off the footpath.

Instead, Connor nods at him, deciding to trust Lachlan can look after himself. 'Take care, huh?'

'Yep, see you Sunday, Ryan,' Lachlan says and steps back from the Patrol.

'If not sooner,' Connor says and pulls away from the kerb, tail-lights washing over the windows of vacated houses on the way out of town.

Still smiling to himself, Lachlan starts down the uneven footpath towards the pub. Jasper Cliff all aglow, every corrugated iron surface warm white gold. A town on the surface of the moon. He realises he loves this place so much – all of a sudden it hurts a little.

When he rounds the corner and sees Glen's ute nudged up against the fence by the bowers, Lachlan doesn't quite know what to make of it at first. He recalls that strange dream-vision he had the first day they met on the Munjina–Roy Hill Road, what he saw as the seizure clobbered him out of nowhere. Glen standing in the gravel, peering out at the Ripon Hills with terrible delight in his eyes. Like a man who had found something so precious and euphoric, he would give up his entire life for it. Just to taste it one more time.

Lachlan tries to shrug this off, but standing here now, seeing the driver's-side door of the ute is wide open, Lachlan senses an odd tautness in the air. As if the lizard corner of his brain has been trying to alert him to something about Glen right from the start. Only his apparent kindness has quelled it.

'Glen?' he sings out. 'You right, mate?'

It plumes in him now, a fusion of epiphany and horror. All adrenaline and instinct. Like nearly stepping on a king brown in the spinifex.

Lachlan circles the ute tray and peers into the cab. He balks at the handsaw sitting in the footwell, completely stiff with drying blood. More of it on the passenger side seat, the driver's seat, on the dash and front windshield. Looks like some kind of impromptu surgery has taken place in here.

His stomach rolls as he glances at the empty verandah, one of the camp chairs pushed over – his. Another swipe of blood, this time on the beam he's leaned against countless times. He approaches the pub's open doorway slowly, strangling the urge to call out Glen's name again.

Hits the light inside to reveal only the scuffed floorboards, his laptop still on the bar, more blood. Christ, he should've grabbed Connor's phone number; he would only be a few k's on the edge of town by now. Surely, he was far more qualified to deal with this shit than Lachlan is.

As he starts edging his way down the hall, every creak and sigh of the old pub threatens to jolt him into a full-on run in the opposite direction. Lachlan wonders what he's about to be confronted with. Can tell there's something dark and bloody just around the next corner, or maybe the next; he just has no clue in what form it will choose to finally show itself. Still a little woozy from the drink, Lachlan finds himself wanting, staggering down the hall to find one of guestrooms wide open. And wondering if he has the strength to withstand whatever is roiling his way with fangs bared and claws reaching.

But after his time traipsing around in the Barite Range, he knows there is some indefatigable drive inside, rooted somewhere at the heart of him and despite the deathly heat, despite his despair and loss, and the loss of so many, that drive still rumbles, compelling him to face whatever waits around the next corner.

Lachlan clears his throat as he sees one of the guestroom doors is ajar. He only feels safe enough to turn on the bedroom light once he can make out the shape of Glen in the double bed, wrapped up in the sheets, paled the colour of marble by the moonlight cutting in through the window.

He should've been expecting this: confusion and terror, endless bloodshed. After all, this is Jasper Cliff. Across the road, the plaques of strange death have inscribed this place's grim history, and can only foretell its future.

Lachlan staggers over to the side of the bed and looks down at Glen's grisly elbow, where most of his arm is missing. He looks peaceful enough, as if asleep, though he's ashen and stiff and can't be anything other than plainly dead. It looks like someone's severed Glen's forearm at the elbow joint with the hacksaw back in the ute and the silly old bugger's stumbled in here to bleed to death on one of Pippa's guest beds.

He blinks down at the gore. *Surely he didn't cut off his own arm?*

He's barely aware of his back clapping against the wall until it stops him in his tracks and Lachlan glances at Glen, lying in this same bed in which Lachlan had slumped just after arriving in

Jasper Cliff for the first time, after Glen had saved him back along Munjina–Roy Hill Road. He forces himself to look away from the tattered meat around Glen's elbow, the white hint of bone showing.

It's only once he's staggered back into the hallway and slammed the door behind him that the most obvious question finally occurs to Lachlan.

The arm, he thinks.

It wasn't in the guestroom and it wasn't in the Triton.

In a half-choked scream, he cries out, 'Where the fuck is the arm?'

The intruder stirs in the red vault of the Rift. It crabs its way from the baking ravine, then reconstructs itself delicately in the gorge on the other side.

Still blood on the little rocks at its feet. After so much horror, witnessed across the hummock grasslands, here but also far, now and since the white men arrived, in the mind-shows of the humans, it barely batted an eyelid to watch the stranger with the hacksaw, in the flesh and hacking at his own flesh. Barely blinked an eye to watch him mutter to himself and then apply the gridded teeth of the hacksaw to his own elbow and then start sliding it back and forth.

It remembers thinking, *Some men truly possess hearts dark as this.* And the simple fact is, the intruder can't show everyone the truth. Many can only see the truth of themselves, not the truth they seek. They peer down into the well and become transfixed by their own reflections, unable to pierce the dark water and see all the way to the ridged and sandy bottom.

The intruder sniffs the scent of blood in the hot, syrupy darkness and wades through the mucky waterhole. It sniffs out into the spinifex until it locates the place where the stranger must've buried his own forearm, rashly and badly. The intruder nudges the spot with its toe-claws and watches the shape of human arm form through the sand with the aid of moonlight.

'*What in all the holy hell are you?*' the stranger had asked, sawing back and forth at himself.

It has almost forgotten – but also the freedom of this. The warm wind peeling off the Coongan River and caressing its scales. Just as sweet as the first time it tasted freedom, once it fled the Afghans and their orders, their harnesses and ropes, a hundred and twenty years ago. It has intruded here far too long, safe and snug in the cusp of hot rock close to the enormous basalt cliff face, which has peered over this land much longer than the intruder has. Time to move on, it decides, turning from the severed human arm in the red sand. Time to search for any surviving siblings, end this long solitude.

The wind refuses to relent, fording the intruder onwards, up through bloodwood and conkerberry, scaring the cattle off towards the station lands, traversing pillow basalt and cracked outcrops, until it gets up onto the high backs of the slopes and can follow the long snaking of the Coongan River. On and on along those banks until time itself is a memory and the intruder is lost in the confluence of red chert and dirty water and warm, sweet earth and all that lies at the heart of Jasper Cliff.

ACKNOWLEDGEMENTS

Each story I write is a love letter to the place from which it emerged. With *Jasper Cliff*, that place is the East Pilbara, in particular the astonishingly beautiful landscape of Marble Bar. The traditional and true landowners of this area are the Nyamal people, and I am honoured and privileged to have been allowed to visit their beautiful country.

I'm sure *Jasper Cliff* would never have made its way out into the world if it wasn't for the support of some very important people. Firstly, the judges of the 2021 Viva La Novella Prize, Jasmine McGaughey and Alice Grundy, who first recognised the worth in this story and highly commended it in that year's competition. Jasmine McGaughey, in particular, gave me some fantastic feedback and guidance in her judge's report on the manuscript.

Georgia Richter is one of the great champions of Western Australian fiction and has long been a supporter of my writing. All through the years I've been sending manuscripts into Fremantle Press for consideration, Georgia always responded with generous feedback and encouragement. She was one of the judges of the 2019 Fogarty Literary Award, for which my unpublished manuscript, *In the Shadow of Burringurrah*, was longlisted.

It was a landmark moment in which I realised I might actually see one of my novel-length stories in print one day – what had long, up until that point, been a pipedream.

Thank you to the judges of the 2022 Fogarty Literary Award, for which this manuscript was shortlisted – Georgia Richter, Brooke Dunnell and Cate Sutherland. Thank you to my writing mentor and PhD coordinator, Donna Mazza, for her unyielding belief in me. To my Aunt Jane, who's been my biggest fan and supporter since I started writing. To the brilliant Kirsten Krauth, who encouraged me to refine what was working in this manuscript, and to jettison what wasn't. To Dawn Mauldon for her invaluable insights into sign language and how Pippa and Aunty Belle would converse. And to my dear friend, Izzie: I suspect our long and morbid conversations about serial killers came in handy when I had to imagine the world from Glen's deranged point of view.

Most of all, I must thank my Mum and Dad. For everything, really. But specifically, for taking me to see Karijini National Park at such a young age and kindling a lifelong obsession with the Pilbara region of Western Australia.

Finally, thanks to the people of Marble Bar, who tolerated me wandering around the streets of their town and along the beautiful Coongan River after my car broke down up there a couple of years back. This story slowly manifested itself along those scorching and mesmeric walks.

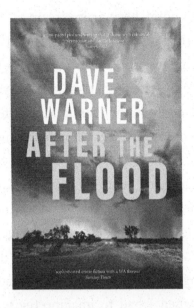

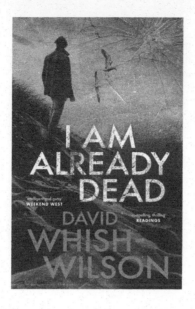